A Tale of an IDIOT and Other Stories

By the Same Translator

Poetry

1. Sentinels of the Soul
2. Melodies of the Broken Reed
3. Rustling Leaves
4. The Invisible Visible
5. Nerves of the Verbal Art
6. Terraced Fields in the Evening Sun
7. Lilacs Lilt in the Lunar Light

Literary Criticism

1. Diversions and Distractions in English Literatures
2. Literary Communion: Critical Essays & Opinions
3. Jayanta Mahapatra: Poet of Unchallenged Fidelity to Art
4. Socio-Cultural Transition in Modern Indian English Poetry and Translation

Short Fiction

1. Cradle of the Dead & Other Stories
2. Full Glare of the Noon and After........(In Preparation)

Novel

1. Ruins in the Palace (In Preparation)

Personality Development

1. Paths to Excellence (In Preparation)

Edited

1. Concerns and Creation (A Critical Study of Mahendra Bhatnagar's Poetry)

(Also wrote Introductions, Forewords, Reviews and critical articles of dozens of books and included in anthologies and published in renowned research journals beside being well-researched)

A Tale of an IDIOT and Other Stories

Translation of Dr. Rajender Toki's
Hindi stories into English
by

R. K. Bhushan Sabharwal

AUTHORSPRESS

Worldwide Circulation through Authorspress Global Network
First Published in 2022
by
Authorspress
Q-2A Hauz Khas Enclave, New Delhi-110 016 (India)
Phone: (0) 9818049852
E-mail: authorspressgroup@gmail.com
Website: www.authorspressbooks.com

A Tale of an IDIOT and Other Stories
(English Translation of Dr. Rajender Toki's Hindi Stories)

ISBN 978-93-5529-131-8

Translator: R. K. Bhushan Sabharwal

Printed in India at Thomson Press (India) Limited

Dedicated in all humility and solemnity to
Supreme Awareness of Infinity:
SAI BABA of SHIRDI
to bless me in the
ETERNAL FLOW to achieve BEYONDING

&

To my most Revered father, Sh. Mohan Lal Sabharwal,
for his being my lasting motivation & inspiration to seek
the brilliance, enlightenment and glory of LOVE & LIFE!

Contents

Foreword

> "A story should be a story; a record of things happening full of incidents, swift movements, unexpected development, leading through suspense to a climax and a satisfying denouement."It should just be a "slice of life", presented suggestively."
>
> –Hugh Walpole

Since 2005, I've had the pleasure of knowing Dr R K Bhushan in a friendship that has progressed beyond ordinary acquaintance to an intellectual partnership. His deep interest in a variety of topics, as well as his significant academic and administrative expertise, have made him an appealing and unavoidable companion of readers. R K Bhushan has made significant contributions to Indian English writing with his seven poetry books, three books of literary criticism and critical essays, a book of short fiction, and a number of forewords, introductions and book reviews. In a book of critical essays, he honestly chronicles his work as a modern critic. Instead of a full-length novel, it's great to watch him develop some different muscles by translating eleven entertaining short stories.

It's a blessing to me to be able to contribute a foreword to his book. When I first started reading R K Bhushan's *A Tale of an IDIOT & Other Stories,* which is a translation of Dr R. S. Toki's short story collection *Shraadh & Other Stories,* I was struck by how beautiful his literary translation was. Translation allows literature to travel, which means that writers can speak across generations and cultures. Bhushan achieves a delicate balance between being true to the original work while also creating something new and unique that evokes the same thoughts and sentiments. *A Tale of an IDIOT & Other Stories* strengthens and benefits Indian writing in English, as a translated work, introducing new vocabulary and concepts. It's all about capturing the spirit of the original Hindi stories without literally translating them. The interplay between time, sentiments, place, and people is explored compassionately and expertly in this collection.

Throughout this collection of eleven short stories, Bhushan explores and subverts deeply ingrained prejudices held towards Indians. The themes include the collision of old and new worlds, the coexistence of modern rituals and traditional ideologies. This book doesn't sugarcoat or romanticize the experiences of the people who have remained at the periphery of Indian society. It offers an unadulterated version of the reality of oppression and marginalization that is unavoidable. Bhushan himself says, '' Although they are closely and faithfully related to the harsh, bitter and indigestible truth of life with all its hidden and suppressed emotions and passions, yet they make a clean departure from the easy, soothing and pleasing interests and tastes of the general reading public. I have invariably felt that these stories are largely autobiographical.'

The stories told here cover the entire spectrum of the modern era, and they have an uncanny ability to touch your heart. Each of the stories in this collection is unique and separate from the others; they demonstrate the artistic and narrative skills of the authors to an astonishing extent. The bizarre humour, appealing storytelling style, and variety featured in these stories will appeal to readers. As they explore the human heart, readers will travel across time, location, and dreams. The stories will attract, relax, and enchant the readers.

Bhushan delves deeply into the lives of people divided between their Indian identity and the complexities of a new environment. Throughout these stories, common people find themselves in extraordinary situations, at times dark and frightening. He provides a deep cultural insight into the lives of people torn between their Indian identity and the complications of a new environment.

They seek love, fight their way out of pain, and practice being human in the most realistic way imaginable, forming a bond between readers and the people they see on the page. The language is simple yet laced with such wonderful prosaic phrases that you can't help but lose yourself in it. This is, without a doubt, a must-read for anyone venturing into the world of short stories. It is very much worth your time.

Dr Neeru Tandon
(MA, LLB, PhD, DLitt)
Professor and Head, Dept of English
VSSD College, Kanpur

Introduction

Life's but a walking shadow, a poor player
That struts and frets his hour upon the stage,
And then is heard no more. It is a tale
Told by an idiot, full of sound and fury,
Signifying nothing.

– *Shakespeare, Macbeth, Act 5, Scene 5*

Dr. Raghukul Bhushan (R. K. Bhushan Sabharwal) has successfully established his name as a remarkable poet and critic of contemporary times. His contributions to contemporary writing in English are substantially immense and include six poetry collections, three books of Criticism, one book of short fiction, Critical Essays on Modern Indian English Writing and other translations. He has also welded his literary caliber as a dashing translator who has, this time, come up with beautiful English translation of stories by Dr. R. S. Toki. Dr Toki, a celebrated scholar of Hindi Language and Literature, is an intellectual giant with deep knowledge of Urdu and music and has published about 46 books of criticism, poetry, philosophy, culture etc. He has also translated the *ghazals* of Ghalib, Mir Taqi Mir, Daag Dehlavi and Sagar Shifai and has critically analysed Sadat Hasan Munto. His two books have been published by the Sahitya Academy, New Delhi. He has written a book about Swami Vivekanand and Aurobindo Ghosh recently.

As a popular art form story writing has always been more entertaining, educative, and informative since centuries. Story, as a work of art, can inspire readers as it is imaginatively much stimulating and can take them on emotional roller coaster of myriads of feelings and experiences, portrayed through various characters conjuring up different realistic situations of life, by inducing them to wear the character's shoes. *A Tale of an IDIOT and Other Stories* is a kind of literary dedication to Dr Toki. As an English translator Raghukul Bhushan has done a commendable job with the befitting English translation of this anthology of stories, in deftly recreating an ironical and sarcastic of life and character portrayals. Laced with comic effect, aiming at making one aware of the reality of life, stories are penetrating and engaging. He has sustained and kept the aesthetic value of Dr. Toki's work in his (translator's) translation.

A Tale of an Idiot and Other Stories contains eleven stories dealing with the characters from different walks of life caught into bizarre situations and the conflicts. The first story *Our Heroic Idol* satirically deals with the pretentious nature and demeanor of a man who, under the spell of so called western Philosophy, vainly tries to pose his image as 'intellectual', 'philosopher', flaunting the airy prop such as Sartre' Being and Nothingness'. The appearance of the hero and his lighting the cigarette reminds us of typical style of Rajnikantha, the South actor.

The next story *Rickshaw-walla* is a poignant tale of woe and the travail a helpless poor man has to face. The narrative of the rickshaw puller is heart wrenching. The mental conflict of the second character, Mr Mehta also bares a lot about the contemporary man of literary, cut off from the well-being of society. There are also some elements of irony and satire.

The story *Shraaddh* presents a vivid picture of social practice, rites and rituals, cultural customs, and the novel way of replacing the old, useless, stereotyped ideas with new ones, symbolized by the book given as a *dakshina,* to the new Brahmin replacing the ritualistic one. The story is conspicuous for beautiful lines pregnant with profundity of thoughts and social awareness: *"To earn more means more exploitation because earning depends on profit-making and profit is another term for exploitation." It has some Marxist leanings so to say.* References to the book of Nietzsche or Sartre or Camus, discussion on Indianness, false customs and traditions, the importance of caste are remarkable.

In another story *Romancing with the Shadows of the Past*, the writer has described living pain and agonizing condition of a paralytic man, aged 60, due to *deadly disease, forced to become an invalid confined to bed for the rest of life*, mad greed of the parents, first wife Surekha's pathos and the rudeness of his second wife. The emotional juxtaposition is brilliant.

The story *The Image Ideal* describes the incident when Sunderlal was on a journey to Delhi without ticket. Sunderlal idolized his image as a nation-builder. It was only then that he used this image for a ticketless travel. but when faced with his student Mangatrai, the ticket examiner; he undergoes series of mental and emotional upheavals.

The next story *The Spell of Creation* deals with the beauty of the girl and that of the poem submitted by her to the protagonist and the latter's different reactions. Poetic discussions between the two on the art of poetic creation lead to development of love relation and emotional affinity in the guide who had to go with his unfulfilled love, one sided love.

ShrimaanJi! is another brilliant story exposing '*dehlila*' (misuse of physical exploitation), by the HOD. It is sarcastic of research scholar's exploitation. The excerpts from the story hint at the duality of the so-called writers. Taking "*Hindi Critics ' to task for their greater reliance on Western critics instead of referring to the Hindi novels,* the writer *wonders : This tendency has grown so well that sometimes that the criticism of a Hindi novel appears to that of a western critic. This infectious disease is spreading day by day. This is a sign of the mental slavery of Hindi critics. This is the urgent timely need to rid ourselves of this dwarfishness.". Following passages from the story throws sufficient light on the difference between 'kathani' and 'karani' of Hindi critics like Shrimanji –*

'SHREEMAAN Ji began to throw light on the personal life of the Hindi novelists and the disgraceful fall of their character after making shallow references to famous Western litterateurs like Dostoevsky, D. H. Lawrence, Kafka, Camus, Sartre etc. how shameful it is that Upendernath Ashak, married thrice whereas Ageya, Dharamvir Bharati, Mohan Rakesh etc. married twice. Ashak wrote his novels on his wives and others on their beloveds. Ramesh Bakashi has not been able to get over the faithlessness of his beloveds. After his love-affair with Mamta, Ravinder Kalia is settled in family life. After describing in detail the love-escapades of Rajender Yadav and Mannu Bhandari and many other litterateurs, he began to speak about the impact of their love affairs on their job and society.'

Another eye-opening remark:

"Girls suit him more for his campaign of writing books. You know girls from poor families looking for livelihood cannot think of revolting. They forget all after getting job with the blessings of SHREEMAAN JI."

In *Dead to all Shame – the Shameless*, protagonist Shyamlal is shown as pleading his "lies like poverty, family, one-time meal for many days, becoming a sycophant, doing odd job at the place of his Office Superintendent, even offering some money to some". He had "learnt the art of moving on with the borrowings from fellow clerks and friends." With his sweet tongue and tactful lies, with his cheating skills he had understood –

The whole world does so. The whole world is busy looting one another; he is also a part of this world. Then why should he alone be dubbed as a cheat – not the whole world?"

Similarly other stories such as *Amanushi, The Denied, the Deprived & the Destitute*, and most importantly, the longest titular story *The Tale of an Idiot* are significantly rendered and aptly transcreated with the same set-up, locales and the experiences and hence, deserve to be read seriously.

The titular story *A Tale of an Idiot,* being the most important and the longest story of the anthology, has autobiographical elements and deserves to be termed as a novel, the short one, as it has also certain elements of being a novel. Supporting this view the writer has also reiterated – 'If *I sit to write all about his childhood, it is possible that it may turn out to be a complete novel for which I have neither time nor courage'.*

He introduces his protagonist as a dreamer and remarks that *'all are dreamers – some less, some more – then are we all idiots? As a rule, we are – every dreamer is an idiot here or there because knowing that dreams are not a reality, we all are lost in dreams. What else should I call it-if not idiocy? This character has been delineated only for your recreation. Yes, then, our idiot hero was a dreamer all through. He enjoyed all happiness in life only in dreams. He had devoted himself wholly to dreams – first as a matter of love, then as a habit and then as a compulsion.'*

With a bit of information about the protagonist's childhood and family background the writer describes his half-blindness as he had to wear '*glasses bearing 12-numbered for the whole of his life'*. He had a very limited vision. In spite of his weak eye-sight the protagonist transcends all the stumbling blocks and is nosed into the world of Hindi literature. His persona reminds one of Milton. It is rather tragic that the 'Idiot', behind the inferiority and loneliness in him, and of course, the negligence, *had to suffer in his family from his childhood till the last moments of his life.* We get a vivid description of his literary evolution. While reading '*the stories of the greatness of Rama, Krishna, Buddha written in his books and thought he too would become Rama and Buddha. He started weaving this dream. He began imagining his own greatness.'*

In short, the titular story *A Tale of an Idiot* sums up his brave act of attaining the literary riches for all his physical, social, visual and familial hiccups. The story in question really inspires and encourages us to emulate his take on vignettes of life. Come what may, we have to move on, following the inner voice and better us in different ways. If we are firmly determined we can also undertake and execute even a daunting task with equal aplomb but the only thing is that our zest and zeal doesn't lie down or die to the challenges.

Dr. Raghukul Bhushan, on the face of it, has made the most use of his literary caliber and experience in translating each and every nuance of the stories so that these stories can catch the fancy of the readers. He has successfully only transferred the beauty and soul of the original stories by Dr. Toki, in his beautiful translation – *transcreation.* Setting, characters, exposition, Actions, climax, conflicts (external and internal), resolution – all find an outstanding articulation and manifestation in this translational work. As for his translational skills, his translation of the stories must be assessed as accurate, consistent, readable, and of course, intelligible and are sure to be popular among the sensible readers of literature. Let's walk in the shadow of different realities fetched through the translational excellence by Dr. Raghukul Bhushan.

Happy reading!

– **Bhaskaranand Jha Bhaskar***
Mumbai

(Dr. Bhaskaranand Jha Bhaskar is a trilingual creative writer, critic, poet and fiction writer, working in BARC, is presently based in Bombay. He is among the adored and idolized poet-critics of Indian Writers in English and is well-researched. His literary output is astonishing as his realistic vision and serious human concerns are the forte of his writings.)

Preface

This book is the translation of Dr. R. S. Toki's short story book *Shraadh & Other Stories* and has been titled as *A Tale of an Idiot & Other Stories*. This is my maiden venture in the translation of a complete book initiated at the hesitant request of a very dear friend, an eminent scholar of diverse intellectual and cultural creative interests in Hindi, Urdu, Music, philosophy, education and religion, with a truly realistic bent of mind, Dr. R. S. Toki. Since he is among my very few friends – good, sharing, caring, understanding and honestly straightforward – for about four decades, he has every right to prompt, provoke and persuade me for his well-considered literary assignment and I also took some time to take up this challenge reading the first five stories from the book, discussed with him and then began the translation in my own way – on the pages of my clipboard and then typing on my PC to prepare the file and then typing directly on the PC till the finish of the assignment. During this process, I would send the translated pages to the writer in his mailbox for his perusal. Dr. Toki's response was not only highly appreciable but also overwhelming throughout and it took almost three months to complete the assignment and I heaved a sigh of relief! It seemed to be a dream project of Dr. Toki and now it is mine with the dream fully realized!

Translation of short and long prose passages from Hindi and Punjabi into English and vice versa has been a compulsory part of teaching all the degree classes for about four decades. My continuous persistent interest in Urdu, Hindi and Punjabi poetry would sometimes urge me to try translation of some couplets and lines into English. I did and felt frequently that it was not possible to convey truly the content and spirit of the original in the same style in translation. Still the effort continued without any sense of discouragement or despair. It led me to reflect seriously on the translation of the greatest books of the greatest writers from across the whole world for the last so many centuries into other languages from Greek, Latin, French, German, Spanish, Russian, Persian, Urdu etc into other languages; and how this passion and zeal for translation built the glory of human cultures and civilizations in enlightenment age after age. And indisputably these translated works are the most precious treasures of the advancement of MAN! This transfer of creativity further quickened the pace of the absorption, assimilation and synthesis of diverse cultures in the unending process of acculturisation and deculturization with new emerging syntheses. I was fully convinced that translation and transliteration have made tremendous contribution to the enlightenment, growth and advancement and even the unity of mankind. Obviously, these too are the creative activities which have their own motivation, delight and glory in art, language and literature. Today there have emerged a number of theories of translation as an artistic and intellectual and literary pursuit with a greater vigor. Even Sahitya Academy, New Delhi, brings out a journal as Indian Literature in which only the translations of poetry, short stories etc. from regional languages are published. Today even the famous quotes and proverbs are translated into the language of the readers across the globe and posted on the FB every day. I must admit that I am very poor in my acquaintance with such theories and knowledge. So I use and have used my own understanding and experience in this maiden venture to retain the taste and flavor of the original with all my limitations of the knowledge of technicalities and even of Hindi language and literature.

My honest and frankness demand that I should mention here that these stories, in original and in translation, are not meant for the ordinary readers, in their content, spirit and style. Although they are closely and faithfully related to the harsh, bitter and indigestible truth of life with all its hidden and suppressed emotions and passions, relentlessly intellectualized, yet they make a clean departure from the easy, soothing and pleasing interests and tastes of the general reading public. The writer is at his best in consciously or unconsciously intellectualizing the emotions, passions, ideas and situations involving the characters portrayed therein. At the same time, I have invariably felt that these stories are largely autobiographical failing the writer in his hard effort to conceal his identity from his very birth to growth and enviable achievements on the zigzag and crooked course of life acquainting the reader with a pageant of relations and relationships. Since I have known and understood Dr. Toki closely and shared his sensibilities and delicate sensitivities, I have learnt much more about the rejections, dejections, projections and determinations from these stories making him what he is today – among the stalwarts of glorious mankind! However, this may not be the broad face of the genius of Dr. Toki as his genius has many faces that emerge from this pigmy-giant!

Very few are born geniuses in the history of mankind but there are countless abundantly rich geniuses who have achieved the pinnacle of glory and created a really enviable space for themselves by the sheer dint of their courage, grit and resolution in the face of disgusting oddities and obscurities! Dr. Toki is one among these countless! I'm reminded of Shakespeare's words in his romantic comedy *Twelfth Night* wherein Malvolio, a steward to rich Countess, Olivia, says in Act ll, Sc.V – "Some are born great, some achieve greatness and some have greatness thrust upon them." That Victorian Aristotle, Carlyle, says in his famous *Hero As a Man of Letters*-"Genius is infinite capacity for taking pains." Dr. Toki has that "infinite capacity" and has published more than 46 books on criticism of Hindi and Urdu writers, with two books published by the Sahitya Academy, New Delhi, translation of Urdu Poetry of Ghalib, Mir Taqi Mir, Daag Dehlavi, Sagar Shifai, Amir Khusaro, Nazir Akbarabadi and his latest *Urdu ki Pragatisheel Shayari* (Progressive Poetry of Urdu); educational philosophy of Swami Vivekananda, Aurobindo and even culture and religion from literary point of view – and his "infinite capacity" doesn't let him pause or relax even today in spite of his near-blind vision since his birth!!!!

It is in view of these wider perspectives and the breadth of vision in the writings of this living legend, R. S. Toki, I can fairly hope that my translation of his short stories would generate readership in the new area!

Happy reading!

R. K. Bhushan Sabharwal
1757/1, Lane 5-R, Heera Bagh,
Jagraon (Ludhiana) Pb.
March 10, 2022

Acknowledgements

My humble gratitude is to Dr. Neeru Tandan Ph.D, D. Litt., LL.B, HOD, Dept. of English, VSSD College, Kanpur, for readily accepting my request to write the Foreword for this book of translated short stories. She was kind enough to correct the script wherever required.

My same gratitude is to Dr. Bhaskaranand Jha Bhaskar, a tri-lingual youthful creative writer, critic, fiction writer and poet, among the foremost contemporary Indian Writers in English, who has always been graceful to oblige me with his scholarly and highly reflective write-ups for my books. His Introduction to my present book of translated short stories is a result of his serious and philosophical reading of these stories and this has well-adored my venture.

I am thankful to Dr. Shaleen K Singh and Dr. Vandita Dharni for their meaningful pre-publication reviews for this book. Dr. Rajender Toki is also fully deserving of my thanks.

I shall betray myself if I don't express my love for my beloved children – my son Vishal Sabharwal and my daughters, Sheenam and Geetika – who are always my total support in life; and also my motivational force and truly loving friend, Sai Sudarshan Kcherry, CEO, Authorspress, New Delhi, for using his professional artistry in bringing out the beautiful edition of this book.

R. K. Bhushan Sabharwal

1
Our Heroic Idol

The hero of this story stopped at the gate of the hostel, he looked around on all sides and found nobody to welcome him. Even then, thinking that there should be at least somebody to meet him, our hero took out a cigarette tenderly from the pocket of his kurta and put it stylistically in the corner of his lips, Took out a matchbox from his pocket and threw away the first burning matchstick as if it put out on its own. Then he lighted the cigarette with the second stick and leisurely entered the hostel.

While entering the hostel, our hero looked around to find out anyone to recognize him as an intellectual. He happened to see three-four unfamiliar faces approaching. Our hero posed to be carefree with the expression of a philosopher on his face and held Sartre's *Being and Nothingness* in one of his hands in such a manner that those passing by may read the name of the author and the title of the book easily. Our hero had done a great hard work to build his image as an intellectual. So now he had to complete his journey from taking out and lighting the cigarette in the fashion of an intellectual. Now he has to carry in hand widely discussed or being discussed this book of English. Not only this, the sentences from this book have also to be learnt to leave an impression on others. Since the friends around, like other young men of India, had little or no taste for reading, they often befool their friends only by reading the Hindi translation of those novels.

When our hero did not see any familiar face there, he stood before Room No. 7 of Block No.4 while inhaling the puffs of smoke. Our hero knocked at the door and he heard a voice-'Come in'! Our hero carefreely inhaled the smoke of the cigarette and opened the door and entered in. our hero feels bad about the door of his room left open but, in spite of this, he didn't shut the door. Had he done so, his pretension of being carefree, being deeply reflective and forgetful, would have been exposed. So leaving the door open against his will, he moved to the chair.

"Shut the door at least, yaar!" said his friend lying in the bed.

Our hero's heart was fulfilled. He smoked another puff and shut the door. Before sitting in the chair, our hero threw the book of Sartre on the table in suc a way that his friend could see the title and may know which book was that and also may understand that it was not done intentionally. While seated in the chair, our hero was lost in deep reflections while smoking leisurely. Our hero has to force himself to be silent because speaking first leaves a bad impression of his image of being a philosopher.

"You have come at a very appropriate time. Satpal is coming with beer."

"Good." Our hero responded with a light smile. Our hero is known to be a man of few words and he has to be miserly in speech against his will. Most of his responses are in" Yah, hum." He has the reputation of being a philosopher in the hostel.

After some moments, there was again a knock at the door. Then Satpal came in opening the door on his own. Our hero knew Satpal. Satpal also knew our hero as a philosopher. But it was his first opportunity to take beer with him. our hero was of the view that Satpal knew him as he wished him to know. However, it was his inner joy that he had a chance to create his desired impression on him.

Satpal poured beer in three glasses. They began drinking beer with formal 'cheers'. Our hero never tasted beer well. Beer's sour taste was never to his liking. After drinking beer, our hero feels like tasting something sweet or delicious but he has to check himself every time. This hero tries to project himself as 'ultra-modern' before others. How can he be orthodox asking for something sweet. In praise of beer,, he would have come up with a number of concoctions. In the light kick of beer, he would intentionally talk of the philosophy of Western philosophers, come out with the sharp criticism of the novels. Then his friends would begin to idolize him. even beer brings out the best of philosophy in him, they would think.

"What are you thinking, dear? Tell us also something.....!" one of his friends had to utter this sentence and the hero also waited impatiently for this sentence.

Even at that time, he suppressed his strong desire to speak and remain silent to deepen his impression on Satpal.

Again there was silence in the room. Now our hero began to wait with greater impatience for a request to say something from his friend and also to think why he decided to be quiet. The crammed sentences of Sartre's *Being and Nothingness* were uneasily stuck up in his mouth.

"Say something, dear!"

These words of his friend proved a life-saving drug for him but showing no eagerness to speak, he inhaled the last puff of the cigarette and threw it on the ground, crushed it under his feet, took out a new cigarette because he found it difficult to talk philosophy without a lighted cigarette in hand.

Our hero had just put the cigarette in his mouth that there was a knock at the door. This sudden knock disturbed both the friends of our hero. So was he himself. Showing outward indifference, he raised his hand as if some guru was about to bless his disciples. He went calmly to the door. There was a telegram man as he opened the door. It was only his telegram. As a proof of his stoicism, he received the telegram and, intentionally leaving the door open, he shut the door with an exclamation 'oh' and took his seat. Instead of reading the telegram, he gulped some beer. Then he took the unlighted cigarette to his mouth. He gave the earlier treatment to the matchstick, lighted the cigarette with the second and began to enjoy smoking leisurely. Although he was very anxious to read the contents of the telegram, yet he was not in a hurry to waste this golden opportunity to impress his friends. And pretended that, while lost in deep reflections, he had forgotten the telegram.

"That telegram?" Satpal couldn't restrain himself. The sharp look of our hero certainly impressed Satpal.

"Ohhhhhh!" Our hero exclaimed as if he had actually forgotten the telegram. He inhaled two puffs of smoke calmly and then opened the telegram. Reading of a telegram shook him for a while. He felt like crying bitterly. He was about to do so when his eyes fell on Satpal who was looking at him with eagerness. So our hero didn't want to erase his impression on Satpal. It must have a bad impression on a friend sitting Satpal because hardly two years ago, in this very room, with four other friends, he had associated his own philosophy of life with a hero of Albert Camus he had admired also because he didn't remember even the day his mother had died and who had refused to have a last glimpse of his mother. Now crying over the news of his own mother's death would be absolutely customary and unphilosophical act that would mean to destroy his hard-built image for ever.

"Whose telegram it is?" Satpal again asked. Our hero inhaled two long puffs of cigarette to control his overwhelming emotions and said indifferently-

"Nothing in particular. My mother is dead!"

Then he felt that his desired impression on Satpal had begun to deepen.

❖❖❖

2
Rickshaw-Walla

It had rained heavily after many days. No human face was visible anywhere. Mr Mehta was feeling upset. It was almost the time of the departure of the train and he must go by that very train. There was no train after that. Even if it had been there, it would not be possible to travel on a long journey without reservation. Stay in back meant losing the chance to participate in the *Mushayara* tomorrow (Poetry recitation function). He had earned great applause in the last week's *Mushayara* and his head was still intoxicated with that and he was not ready to miss tomorrow's *Mushayara* at any cost. It was after a long time that he had tasted its delight.

Unmindful of the wall created by the rains, this uneasiness led him to the gate. He happened to see a rickshaw at a distance in this rain. His face brightened with this pleasant surprise. His uneasiness and being drenched in rain, he called him. that rickshaw-puller might not have heard his call in the noise of the splashing rain but he stopped exactly near Mr. Mehta.

" To railway station?" Mr. Mehta said hurriedly.

"Sure. Be seated."

"Charges?" Mr. Mehta asked in his feminine expert is.

"Give whatever you will, Sir. It is my first earning of the day." Said the rickshaw-puller wiping his face with the already fully wet his shoulder=cloth.

"Okay! Let us go." Upset by the rains and the train-timing in mind and deciding how much to pay him, Mr. Mehta swiftly entered the rickshaw.

Mr. Mehta felt relaxed as rickshaw moved and he began to caress his ego remembering the applause of last week's *Mushayara.* He was hearing the dual sound of the rainfall and he felt lost in himself. The rickshaw was moving unbearably slow and Mr. Mehta took it as a blessing of the rains. In this mood, he didn't care for the jerks created by the rickshaw-puller's forced paddling, crying and his hand repeatedly pressing his knee on one side.

"What is the matter, baba?" Mr. Mehta asked.

"What should I say, Sir?" painfully crying rickshaw-puller said, "I am pulling the rickshaw with a passenger after so many days. But this knee...." He forced push the paddle with a right foot with a cry. The passenger noticed for the first time that his right knee was bandaged. So his hand was repeatedly pressing the knee.

"If you are in deep pain, I can get down." Mr. Mehta said in a lifeless tone. Rickshaw was moving at a snail's pace and the station was still far away; he won't be able to walk fast on this flooded road. So he kept sitting with a feeling of helplessness. Then the cars and scooters passing by will delight in splashing water on him.

"Oh, no, babuji, you keep sitting. Bless O God!" rickshaw-wallah replied in pain. After a silence of few moments, pulling the unbalanced rickshaw, he said again with a painful cry-

"You have appeared like a god, Babuji. There is nothing left to eat at home. This is the time to starve. I have a little son. How can I see him starving. O God, you alone can bless! Babuji, I met with a car accident. Leaving me unconscious on the road, he drove away. Some people took me to the hospital. Some days later, a doctor told me that my right leg would have to be amputated. I ran away from there. O my god! Reached home with great difficulty in pain. God has created sufferings only." He felt difficult to speak even. He pressed his knee again with his hand to relieve himself of pain. He began again with a cry," Since then, I am at home. Neither knee-pain gives me relief, nor the wound is healing. For some days, lived on one meal a day! Even that is not possible now."

"You are in great pain. I may get down." Mr. Mehta felt that he would walk faster to his destination and the railway station as not very far.

"No sir, you keep siting. Railway station is not very far." Rickshaw-puller said in a tone of cry.

"How long it would go like this?" Mr. Mehta muttered looking at his watch. The rickshaw-puller, without understating the uneasiness of Mr. Mehta, said-

"As long as it goes! God bless Dr. Ramnath who has assured curing it without amputation. O god, he opened the stitches, filled the gaping wound with some ointment and then bandaged it. A poor man can't rest. There is nothing at home to eat. Had to come out in the rain." He paused and began crying again.

Mr. Mehta looked at his knee unwillingly. The bandage was drenched in rain. Perhaps some blood was oozing out there and the bandage was coloured saffron. Mr. Mehta had a feeling of nausea. He looked away from there and tried to reflect. Then he heard him muttering," God's Will! Not many days to go!"

Suddenly, the rickshaw stopped. Mr. Mehta was upset. "What happened?" escaped his mouth.

"Nothing Sir, The chain came off." He stopped the rickshaw on the roadside and went to the rear. Mr. Mehta became restless. He was looking at his watch again and again and he could hear him crying. He was finding it difficult to bend. Somehow rickshaw moved forward and Mr. Mehta heaved a sigh of relief that rickshaw was moving at least.

At the turn of the rickshaw, the red building of the railway station was in sight. At this, Mr. Mehta felt new life in his veins. Rains became faster before he could get down. But he got down hurriedly. Took out money and gave one rupee in excess in his large-heartedness and he saw that without any grudge, the rickshaw-puller accepted the money gratefully touching it with his forehead and rickshaw handle and put it in his pocket. While running towards the railway station, he noticed that the blood oozing out of his knee flowing in line over his leg was dissolving in the water in a long red line and fully drenched in the rain and shivering rickshaw-puller was beckoning at the prospective passenger.

❖❖❖

3
Shraaddh*

After presiding over a seminar in Delhi, I had returned home badly tired early in the morning by the night train. I had a plan to stay in Delhi and meet some scholars there. But I received my wife's message on mobile from home urging me to return home as it was the *shraaddh* of dear mother that day and she had arranged to feed the Brahmins exactly at eleven. She didn't forget to tell me on mobile to stay hungry. I had no any particular interest or faith in *shraaddh* but an intellectual like me felt spineless to decline the urge of my wife. So I had returned home without eating anything during the journey. Like the practice followed every year, she well-prepared the *thaal* with kheer and poories and asked me to serve the same to Panditji. As always, without any kind of arguments, I carried out her command. After I was free from this half-an-hour ceremony, I went to my room to check my mail – there were some invitations – like shraaddhs, there is a season of seminars also.

I was still in the midst of doing with the mail, that somebody's footsteps drew my attention to the door. I saw Raghu standing there. I had a mixed feeling of surprise and joy on seeing him, and suddenly – "O, Raghu, you?" – escaped my mouth.

---

* An annual ceremony observed by Hindus to feed the Brahmins to show their respect and belonging to their dead ancestors in the family.

Raghu shook hand with me and sat in the chair beside me. Raghu's dirty wrinkled clothes, unkempt hair, beard grown for many days which made his already brown complexion more brown, which might have annoyed some aesthetician but it was all easily acceptable to me, the reason was that, in spite of his being a mere matriculate, Raghu could expose the intellectual bankruptcy of any known intellectual on the strength of his studies. It was an intellectual delight to talk to Raghu, and his greatest quality was that he not only discussed intellectually but also lived it.. that was the main cause of his impoverished life also. He would say-"To earn more means more exploitation because earning depends on profit-making and profit is another term for exploitation."

He had followed it fully in his own life. When he felt that he had earned enough for daily needs, he would shut his spare-parts shop and return home to occupy himself sometimes with the book of Nietzsche or Sartre or Camus. He who had spent all his past earnings on books was Raghu and he would spend all pension money of his dead father on books even today. That is why, Raghu had no friend to say so – studies had made him an introvert – and if he had any, he was not in a position to invite them to his home. I was the only one left who, with all his snobbery, would sit in the wooden chair comfortably in his one-and-a half room residence. That was perhaps the only reason that he treated me respectfully and also felt emotionally attached with me. However, it was rare and he came.

"Say, how are you, yaar? You have come after so many days." I said with complete informality.

"I am fine. Had a mind to see you for many days, so I came today." He said with a smile. Then he paused and said – "I have a request to make."

"Of course, come out with it."

"Will you come home with me?"

His proposal seemed strange to me for a moment but that was not important for me.

" Yes, why not?" I said.

"So get ready."

"I am ready – returned from Delhi a while ago."

"Then you must be tired?" he said with a little disappointment.

"Nothing to bother. Let's go." With my hand on his shoulder, I said.

Informal discussion started on Indianness while we were riding a scooter. The discussion moved on to false customs and traditions and stopped at the importance of caste. Both of us emphasized *Karma-based* caste. We might have felt more provoked in this discussion but the scooter had to be stopped before his home.

He unlocked the door and led me in. what a room it was, stacked madly with books like a godown. Books on different writers and subjects were lying at the whole place. I sat in the only chair in the room and threw a casual glance at the books. He began by talking about new books and then on those he had read, and then – "I will just return" – saying this, he went to the adjacent room which was all in one – store, kitchen, and what not? I began to turn the pages of the books.

Few minutes later, he brought kheer, curd and poories in a plate. I cast a questioning glance at him and he said-"It is the shraaddh of dear mother today." Before I could say something, he said," I know you are not a Brahmin by caste. But, in my view, you are a true Brahmin; Brahmin means a very learned person only, isn't it? So from this point, there can't be a truly greater Brahmin than you. What have I to do with such

Brahmins as are karamheen and brainless." I understood Raghu and I smiled. I was about to say with a laugh "When did you start believing in these rituals?", he came out with-" This is the first shraaddh and it concerns mother. Mother is related to mind and emotions. So I have done this all. Couldn't find another learned Brahmin in this city, only you I could think of." Raghu silenced me. I was full of praise for him in my heart because sharing his ideological approach, I could even reject the ritualistic Brahmins. I had never been able to rise above such customary sanctions. Raghu had risen very high in my eyes. To lighten the seriousness of the conversation, I asked mischievously, "Then what are you offering as *dakshina* to this Brahmin."

"I have brought this new book for this purpose. Hopefully you like it." Eagerly he replied.

I had a spoonful of kheer and his face had the same expression on his face that a devotee has while feeding a Brahmin! (*Khee*r is a dessert specially made by boiling rice in milk till it is thick and added with sugar and dry fruits by choice.)

❖❖❖

4
Romancing with the Shadows of the Past

He had never hoped that his active life would meet such an end. He had been so busy with the hurry and worry of life that he didn't know that he would badly suffer from this deadly disease and he would become an invalid confined to bed for the rest of life. His right side had become completely paralytic and it was difficult for him to move. As a result, his life of haste and waste had come to a standstill. He was experiencing living pain. Rest for a few days is a different matter but the agony of this very condition in future was increasing. God be thanked that he had enough money and means that he could employ a whole-time servant to take his full care. He was paying for neglecting his health.

This added to his suffering when somebody came to inquire about his health saying with a deep sigh-"Who knows of which bad deeds you are bearing this punishment today! You are only sixty." He would say ditto to them but in his heart of hearts, he was aware of the sin he had committed in his youth.

The memory of that incident that caused this life-long suffering was haunting him while he was confined to bed and no effort could jerk it away. He would try to divert his mind but his past continued to haunt him. it was more painful to live with the memories with this paralytic body. He had been begging for death in these two months only because that innocent face he could hardly forget stared at him every moment. He was unable to check the appearance of that incident on the scale of his memory and that troubled him a lot. He had never thought the greed would lead him into this dreadful agonizing situation. But it was not his fault – it is a result of that malefic influence of the family on him that he is experiencing today and he couldn't foresee then.

How happy he was in marrying that innocent and simple girl of a few words. She was a submissive wife to obey him. He couldn't understand the rude and cruel temperament of his mother and the unbridled greed of his father then. Their temperament was all for him. so he couldn't realize the calm silence and the deepening sorrow on his wife Sulekha's face. Being the only child, his parents were supreme for him. So he was used to see everything through their eyes and delighted in speaking their language. Sulekha brought in dowry all that a girl from an ordinary middle class family could bring but what could be done with the mad greed of the parents. She endured silently the harsh tongue of the mother and did all the work of a housewife. She would clean the utensils, wash the clothes, clean the house and did the cooking calmly without a grudge. But sadness was writ large on the face of this calm Sulekha which he took as her arrogance and her authoritative posture in those days. In those days, he didn't have much business and it was the time of economic hardship – he had inherited the greed from his parents and he had begun to discuss money matters with Sulekha hinting money from her parents.

When Sulekha did nothing even after many hints and she kept doing her daily home work, he and his parents took it as Sulekha's cunning in those days. In spite of being abused and beaten, she didn't react and did or said anything mean and low. She did weep secretly but she never shed tears before anybody to beg or did any work resentfully. Mother took it as her obstinacy – she also felt it like that but it was not so – but she learnt it later.

Then her indifference was her intentional obstinacy freedom from which was becoming necessary every day. All her virtues became her vices and an eye-sore to all and this piercing pain became unbearable.

One day, she sought mother's permission to do laundry in the washing machine. Mother also gave her a huge heap of clothes to wash and he went to the shop with his father as usual. Then the inevitable happened as expected. She died of the electric current. There was a chaos at home. Sulekha's parents helplessly drank the bitter draughts and he himself was overjoyed at his riddance from Sulekha coming safely out of this mishap. No one suspected him. if Sulekha's family had any suspicion, they could say nothing and to whom? They had no way except to endure silently.

The virtues and goodness of Sulekha began to light upon him after the second marriage. He got handsome dowry in spite of his second marriage because the father of the second wife was a rich merchant and he made him a partner also in his business. That was the reason that he was able to accumulate so much wealth. His mother and father were very happy. He too was happy to begin with. But his wife started showing her true colours as time passed and he felt suffocated because he feeling the pressure of the wealth of his father-in-law. His wife was sharp-tongued and she passed her time, not doing anything, but in finding fault with the work of the servants at home. She would dominate the mother also. The birth of a son heightened her arrogance. In such a suffocating situation, the thought of Sulekha caused him more pain and misery. The well-maintained home of Sulekha had become a junkyard now. Nothing was in place. He began staying away from home, spending more time in business and started drinking in excess to be forgetful of the innocent sad face of Sulekha. His mother died of heart-ailment and now she became the governess of home. His father was killed in the rail accident in Bombay. And he was left to himself.

His son was under the control of the mother and went abroad for studies at last – and didn't return after that – got married there. This hurt his mother so badly that she too was confined to bed. Now she remained busy in hurling abuses at the servants. One day, she went to sleep, never to wake up again!

The memory of Sulekha continued to haunt him amidst all these mishaps. Sometimes, he felt she was cleaning and dusting, sometimes she was arranging his clothes carefully, sometimes looked at him with loving admiring eyes and sometimes, her sad wet eyes shook his inner being. He would remember all her virtues one after the other adding to his yearning and languishing. The meanness of his own deeds began piercing him to escape which he would drink more and more. He was left alone to endure the pains and pangs with the servants around. The shadows of the past had started haunting him. he couldn't run away from them, even if he willed so. He felt as if nature had made him paralytic and confined to bed. And the shadows of the past, like a serpent with its hood out, was about to bite him and there was no way but to endure. Then he had escaped the punishment but now he couldn't escape this life of extreme suffering and agony with no remedy. Repentance and bearing endless pain alone were his destiny. Life had slipped out of him!

❖❖❖

5
The Image Ideal

Sunderlal took two rounds of the train compartment and then assuring himself that there was none known to him, he sat quietly near the window seat. The train was crowded and the compartment was full in no time. When the train whistled and moved, Sunderlal placed his bag on the seat, had a quick round of the compartment and sat again with a sense of satisfaction on his seat.

Sunderlal was a little upset today, he was not travelling without ticket for the first time. It had become his long-settled habit as he was used to it for long now. But he could make little use of this habit, he would make the best use of his journey only from one station to the second or third station. But it was for the first time that he was going to Delhi alone and in spite of his talkative wife's hard persuasion, he had not bought a ticket as was his habit.

Nobody knows why Sunderlal developed this habit; when he began the job of a school master, this habit was perhaps rooted then. Being miserly by nature and always flattering himself that school masters are the nation-builders, he would often tell others that all school master should be allowed free rail travel anywhere. When nobody else took even the least trouble of listening to him, he allowed himself this concession. When he was to go to his village after a week or two, he would travel by a passenger train. Bus travel would cause nausea in him. train travel was comfortable to him. Helpless by habit, Sunderlal would remain cautious that he didn't see any familiar person. And he often succeeded in his mission as there are many compartments in the train whereas this facility is not available in the bus.

But this time, he was a little disturbed and worried – the journey was long and there was every possibility of the ticket examiner coming and he would be caught. Sunderlal idolized his image as a nation-builder. It was only then that he used this image for a ticketless travel. Sunderlal was not thick-skinned like other ticketless travelers who were least bothered when caught. He did go to the ticket window, reached his pocket for money to buy ticket but he lacked courage. Some people greeted him also and he too joined the crowd moving to the train.

There was a rush in the train and Master Sunderlal felt pained on such occasions that the school master had lost his identity in this new society. Otherwise also, man today is so badly confined within himself that he has no time to know anybody around or move with him. but when he was not in train, he nursed a deep grudge that this society doesn't even recognize the nation-builders, what to speak of showing respect to them. He often complained about this. He never felt opposition to his views.

The train had just passed two or three stations that Sunderlal's hearbeat fastened. The ticket-examiners had entered the compartment. A short-statured ticket-checker was examining the ticket of a passenger sitting beside him and suddenly stopped while extending his hand to Sunderlal for a ticket and eagerly said-

"Oh, Sir, you? Namaste dear Sir!" saying this, he happily bent forward to touch his feet. Stunned Sunderlal was watching this short-statured youngman in surprise. He had never found himself in such an awkward situation. But what did that short man know about the awkwardness of Sunderlal or what is passing in his mind. Feeling that 'Sir' has not recognized him, he said-

"Have you not recognized me, sir? I'm Mangatrai, your mischievous student."

"Ohhhhhhhh." Sunderlal spoke as if he was trying to breathe. What else he could say. Every teacher recognizes his student when introduced. The passengers sitting around had their eyes fixed on them and the word 'mischievous' brightened their faces. Mangatrai was damn happy on being recognized by the masterji. He addressed the other passengers sitting beside masterji-

"Sir was our best teacher. He rebuked us very much, taught us well, and was also highly affectionate. I enjoyed his special favour. 'Sir', you are going somewhere? Tell me if I can be of some help." The passengers had appreciative looks Sunderlal would have been proudly overjoyed, if it had been another occasion and spoken high of this brilliant naughty student for many days to all adding his spicy lies. But now he felt troubled like a bird caught badly in the cage but trying a natural smile on his face. What if he asks for a ticket? Will any lie save him? what will become of his image of being a nation-builder? He decided not to tell Mangatrai about his going to Delhi. But what else to say? Something stuck in the throat of Sunderlal. As he reached his pocket to take out his handkerchief, Mangatrai said, "Leave it, Sir. It is fine."

In the meanwhile, another ticket-examiner reached there and beckoned Mangatrai to move. While checking the tickets of other passengers, Mangatrai said, "OK, Sir. Just coming after five minutes after finishing the job. Want to talk a lot to you."

Taking out his hankey and covering his mouth, he coughed and shaking his head, said, "Achha!" He felt back to life after Mangatrai had left-his heartbeat was still fast. "Do you find such brilliant students as respect so much their teacher?' Sunderlal heard and looked at them. Some passengers were still casting admitting looks at him. once he felt that he should utter some false praises about this naughty student. But Sunderlal felt more troubled with his identity and the image created by Mangatrai. He had forgotten the concession he had given to himself as a nation-builder and regretted having ignored the advice of his talkative wife. He could foresee the happenings to come. This disturbed him to think of the opinion of the other passengers if he were caught. Sunderlal was indecisive. Then the train slowed down. May be there is a station. Sunderlal picked his bag hurriedly. The train had not yet halted, ready to get down at the door, Sunderlal happened to see Mangatrai coming in front.

"Oh, Sir. You are going? You were to alight here only?"

"Han……." said the confused Sunderlal."

"Okay, Sir. Namaskar. Tell me if I can do anything. I'm in this train only." Said Mangatrai touching Sunderlal's feet.

Sunderlal took no time in getting down as the train stopped. He heaved a long deep sigh of relief as if he had escaped from the jaws of death.

❖❖❖

6
The Spell of Creation

"Beautiful girl and a poem! Impossible!" this was exactly my reaction when that beautiful girl had given her beautiful poem for the first time to me for correction. My position was like this-" Sometimes I look at her and sometimes I look at her poem." My first reaction was on my experiences in many poetry recitation functions that this beautiful girl has used some *shayar* to compose a poem on her beauty. But this assumption of mine proved wrong later. Her beauty was spell-binding and so was her poetry. Undoubtedly, this seeming imaginary beauty was a living reality in my life and I was helpless in enduring this double hurt. She was not only the sculpted image of Ajanta Caves but she herself was a sculptor of such idol with her enchanting words. She had a unique passion for such poetic creation. Her own charming beauty and her poems were quite forceful to create the feeling of inferiority in a balanced sane person. I was already engaged in this – so a poet I was – seeing her enhanced that inferiority in me and I began writing more and more poems. It was my good luck that she accepted me as her guru whose dream of marrying such a Venus was getting older. Love for her began to flow indirectly in my life and directly in my poetic compositions. Brighter glow began to appear in me and my poetry.

She would come to show her poems to me and sit for hours talking on a variety of topics like Hindi poetry, Urdu poetry and its technical forms etc.; sometimes about poetic creation and the blind beliefs, evil customs etc of this orthodox society. In all her conversation, her main role was that of a curious questioner and mine of the god Rajnish. She would keep looking at me with her fixed big eyes whereas I continued my sermon in the typical style of Acharya Rajnish. I knew that this technique had the effect of opium on the people, especially women. That is why she often appreciated me saying that I was a good orator to convince others of my viewpoint. I would thank Rajnish lavishly in my heart of hearts for teaching me not only this unique art of speaking and heaps of speaking material and would offer millions of thanks to God that this beauty had never heard or read Rajnish. Or this would have exposed me. Although there was no such need – the material of Rajnish was sufficient – yet I started reading books on the art of poetic creation so that she stays under the spell of my impression so that she remains mesmerized by my originality even if she ever reads or listens to Rajnish. In an effort to keep my impression, I would make some formal corrections in her well-written poems. Sometimes I wouldn't do so lest she should know my cleverness. I would often admire her beauty in my heart of hearts and her poems with my words on hearing which another layer of confidence in her and inferiority in my spread. She often asked – "You write so well. Why don't you publish your books?" on hearing this from her, I would try to create pity in like a languishing Devdas with some success – after all she was from a middle class family."

I got her one or two poems published in magazines to keep alive my image of being a guru. In spite of repeated requests from the publishers, I didn't give her photograph to be published and retained it with myself to delight in loneliness. The publication of her poems excited her then my Monalisean smile brightened in my pure middle class style. I was completely mad in her one-sided love till the publication of poems. I would write a poem on her and feel her presence in her absence. Her coming would glow the moments. We had become friendly by then and had a feeling of frankness also. But I was not able to rise above my middle class hesitation about this one-sided love. Fear of losing her was my greatest weakness. So didn't say my mind in this matter and my sermons continued. But the day she told me that her parents were eager to marry her off while she was unwilling, my nights became sleepless. I started provoking her again the institution of marriage. I wanted her to suffer from marriage-phobia somehow. I would awaken her to her superb intelligence and convince her that marriage would ruin her talent. Then I would convince her with the examples of a host of poets and writers whose genius was crushed in marriage and how they could keep alive their creativity by ridding themselves of their wives. Then I convinced her that creativity is the greatest bliss. She should not make a mistake of sacrificing the joy of her creative genius on the narrow and conservative happiness of married life. Only very rarely, people enjoy the superb quality of a forceful creativity. He who is gifted with this, he must use it to the best advantage of remarkable creations and join the clan of immortals. What is the fun of bearing four or five children in marriage to die unknown? He who wastes the diamond-like precious creative talent on the sands of the marital bliss is a fool. What do we gain by dissolving nectar in poison?

Although the mad passion had been put off for a while in her refusal to her parents, yet I continued my ant-marriage campaign to keep my own interests safe. I would work hard on the cases of unhappy marriages from her own mohalla and that of mine to prove to her the futility of marriage. At the same time, I started looking for a job on war-footing. The reality of all arguments against the institution of marriage was that she should not agree to marry till I was in job. I myself wanted to marry that Venus sooner I got a job. I was quite sure that she won't refuse to marry me when I got a job, and if she did, I had the capability to persuade and convince her of keeping alive her poetic creation.

I had to request and beg the editors to publish some of her poems to ensure her refusal. But the real problem was of getting a job which seemed to be my lot only after the age of retirement. I constantly felt the danger of losing that figure of Ajanta as I was fully acquainted with the psychology of the Indian parents. I lost not only my appetite but also it slowed down my poetic creativity in this tension. My inability often irritated me. I often was in a mood of "burn and blow into flames this world." I admit that all the poems I composed in those days were under the larger influence of Faiz and Sahir. What else could I do? No job and I was losing my life. Faiz and Sahir alone were the only mean of catharsis in such a situation. At last I decided to relieve myself of this tension by sharing with her my one-sided love. I began to wait for her.

One day she came and informed me that her marriage had been fixed with a foreign-returned doctor. My tender and sensitive heart broke into pieces. But I congratulated her hiding all my pain in the style of film heroes. I regretted of having lost a disciple, she bowed her head in the typical style of a middle class girl. I expressed the hope that she would continue to compose poems. After she was gone, I wept bitterly like a middle class young boy and grew my beard in this sad situation. My condition in those days was "I shall die weeping in the pangs of separation from you." This liberated my paused creativity with an uncontrollable flow. " stay you happy is my prayer" branded the flood of my poems. Number of poems kept rising relieving me of my sorrow and I began to gain normalcy.

There she became an alien and here my being in job left me to my parents. No amount of persuasion by the parents could bind me in the bonds of solemnized marriage. I loved to be in a situation – I shall wait for you till doom's day! As such I kept on writing poems on the pangs and pains of loneliness, sadness and that callous love. Thus I had a collection of poems. Since I was employed now, and could spend money, I accepted all the conditions of the exploitative publisher and began to finalize the script of my poetry collection. I excluded most of the lyrics and set out to write a long introduction on the "Art of Creation." Whatever persuasions I had used for her were also here and I created the illusion that she would know my love for her on reading this. I explained poetic creation as the most significant creation and the impact of its pain most indispensable. Whatever bliss is there in the world, it is the bliss of creation. I cited the examples of great sages of the world to support my viewpoint. I had read all these views from the voluminous books covered with the thick layers of dust to convince her to save herself from the pleasures of marriage. To be brief, I happened to write a long research article on the process of creativity which made my book look like a book otherwise the book with sixty songs in sixty pages would have been good for the children of first standard.

The book was published and gifted to friends. Not my poems – they all unanimously admitted the influence of Bachchan and Mahadevi – of course, my introduction became a subject of hot discussion and I didn't lose anything, though the gains were many. The first was that I became the centre of discussion and popular too. Secondly, this controversy encouraged the hot sale of my book. Thirdly, I began to write with greater force in defense against the staunch critics of my introduction. Lo! I started working on another book! Fourthly, I had to study hard to beat my critics as a result of which my scholarship began to hold firm grounds. In fact, the critics were not prepared to admit that poetic creation alone is the finest and supreme creation. Some so-called poets regarded it as a second-rate creativity. Such orthodox atheistic poets would regard God alone as the Highest Creator. In an effort to respond effectively to their stupid arguments, I became oblivious of the pain of separation from her. When did I become a critic from a poet in this process, I didn't know even? Perhaps there was a strong desire in my unconscious to appear as a doctor before her doctor-husband. I wanted her to realize that whom she had lost was also a doctor.

This suppressed desire in my unconscious had suddenly raised its head and I started research work. The job of a school teacher also continued with this.

One day when I returned home, I learnt that she had come with the promise of coming again in the evening. The paused emotions again began to revive, though I was aware of its futility. Since this was the first and only love, it's gasping pain was still there. I wanted to gift my signed book to her with the remarks that she could realize her mistake on reading it and weep and then I would play an important role of a side – hero. But when I was not satisfied with any thought-out line, I decided to write spontaneously when she comes. I placed the book on the shelf. I placed the recently published book with my article on creation on the table because she would often sit in the adjacent chair there and from there she could easily pick and see everything. I would have kept open that very page where my article begins, if I could! But it was not possible because then she might not have seen that poem on which rested all my hopes and which was one of the rejected poems while I was preparing my poetry collection and were lying there corrected.

I was shocked when she came. I was left with a deep cold sigh on seeing her beauty more brightened. That fair-complexioned body could have been mine also if I had not lost it in my cowardly sadness and pain. This charming body can still be mine in case her husband deserts her or dies. I wish it could be possible! Then I would have gone fighting against the social conventions to marry this spongy bodied divorcee or widow though I was a *sanskaari.* She had a plumpy beautiful child in her lap whom she laid informally on my bed and herself also sat there. I felt puzzled at this all. This innocent villain had already failed all my plans and then there was an imminent danger of his wetting my bed which my aesthetic sense was not prepared to accept. I helplessly sat in the chair she was to sit in after she sat in the bed. She began to enquire about my well-being. Feeling happy with one or two of my lies, she started telling me about herself. I tried unsuccessfully to trace a sign of sadness, sorrow or deficiency in her life in her narrative. She began to shower lavish praises on her husband and unconsciously rubbing salt on my wounds. When her recitation of "pati-puran" crossed all limits of my tolerance, which was clearly for a short time, I lost control and got up from that chair. During her recitation and moving towards the bookshelf for my collection of poetry book, I asked – "Did you write any new poem or some new creation?"

" Had no time for all such things. Yes, whatever creation, good or bad, I could do, is before you." She said with a little shyness.

" Where is it?" I turned eagerly towards her with my poetry collection in hand. I felt a lucky card had fallen in my hand.

"Here it is." She pointed towards that innocent villain. "This is also creation. I have created a living being. I have created a living poem. Is it not a poem, not a creation?"

She hurled the question at me in her old style. I was scared at the sight of glow, self-confidence and sense of satisfaction on her face as she explained. I could have fought the battle of words with the critics but I had no tools to fight the situation of 'truth before needed no proof." I hid my poetry collection between the magazine and the poem lying on the table and was seated tired in the chair. I began to be scared of her comfort and felt the uselessness of arguing with her. I was feeling lifeless before her glow, self-confidence and complacence. I was just about to say something when my sleeping foe began to cry and saw that he was wetting the bed and also spreading some other creation there. That day after that beauty left, the first thing I did was to give my consent to my parents so that her creation addresses me as maternal uncle and my creation addresses her as paternal aunt to create relief for me.

❖❖❖

7
Shrimaan Ji-?!!!

I received a message from the Head of the Dept. to meet him when I reached the department to take my class. I was told on meeting him that the well-known Marxist Hindi critic, Shrimaan Ji, was visiting here next week to deliver a talk on the latest status of Hindi novel. When I told the HOD that I finished my study of the writings of Shreemaan Ji only last week and I have reached the conclusion that the Marxist influence is visible only on his first book, not on the rest, this created another layer of my scholarship and studies on his mind. As always, he asked me to write something on the complete works of Shreemaan Ji for him. Before I could say-"I will write just now" – he asked me "to complete my write-up in a day or two" – and saying this he pretended to be busy with his work and I came out.

In fact, whenever some well-known scholar or writer visits here, then usually I am asked to give my write-up on his works. I have been doing this job in the presence of that very HOD with some exceptions. But now I don't do that because, after tolerating me doing this job three or four times, the HOD had been attuned to "give me your write-up in two-three days." He wanted to create an illusion for himself that an immature student like me doesn't have complete knowledge of that scholar. Whenever he felt dwarfish before a scholar, he took advantage of his promising and highly brilliant student to face that scholar for discussion and seeing my impact on that scholar, he had a feeling of self-satisfaction. If such incidents gave an opportunity to learn something, it made me arrogant also. I couldn't rid myself of this feeling in spite of my self-awareness because the other professors of the department won't give a chance for this. This arrogance didn't let me accept the humble requests of my fellow students to correct their poems. As a result, these young girls expert in humble requests started taking interest in my fellows.

Here I have no hesitation in frankly admitting one thing. Whenever the constant devotee and staunch supporter of Indian culture, our HOD, with the help of his half grey hair and the word 'daughter' combining with the fatherhood, has caressed the body of a beautiful girl in his embraces as if he has been doing research on some innovation in Indian culture, then I also felt some provocation. I felt also to push him aside to do the innovation myself. I feel greater excitement when the HOD invites some beautiful girl doing research to his residence after seven regarding research to transform that oral research into practical research. Truly speaking, watching this all, I also feel tempted to be a professor in a PG college after completing my research.

I am the first to break the long tradition of enchanting "Gold Medalist" beauties in this department continuously doing innovation in Indian culture. My two research articles which were published in two reputed journals sometime after my joining M. A. are credited for my performance. The psychological effect of my articles on the professors of the department was such that they couldn't help giving me the maximum marks while evaluating my answer books. These learned professors have expressed their generosity to me many times with this lie that my answers have deeply moved them whereas the truth is that I don't know what answers I wrote in my egoism. In the meanwhile, I was the first Gold Medalist and it was also for the first time those female students were annoyed with me who couldn't be successful even after the 'rightful use" of the weakness of the professor. They had taken my triumphant success as humiliation of their beauty and youth. In fact, whatever enviable credit my professors impressed by my critical research articles had shown to the people, this was the only way with them to prove it. Otherwise also they couldn't risk the truth being exposed to all by giving high marks to their foolish shishya (girl student). Undoubtedly both were irritated at their inability to cash in on their '*deh lila*' (misuse of physical exploitation). They also suffered extreme agony while allowing me admission to M. Phil Course which they described as their finest good luck that a brilliantly promising student was there in the department.

I gave my write-up on all the books of SHREEMAAN Ji to my HOD after two-three days. As always, this time also, he asked me questions on the subject of the literature of SHREEMAAN JI as if he had read SHREEMAAN JI and now he was asking me questions just to refresh himself about the writings of SHREEMAAN JI and also know if I had read SHREEMAAN JI seriously. But this is not the truth. It is because he presents all that I tell him with his own layer of Indian Culture on my material. I also never gave false information to the HOD. I do call it my honesty but the fact is that it is my smartness or cunning. I don't want to minimize my impression the HOD in any way. I have suggested to him twice or thrice my fundamental and well-argued views about the writings of one or the other well-known Hindi litterateur that he earned great appreciation by writing on them. In reality, it is also extremely to be cunning to be a Gold Medalist in M. Phil. It is also extremely essential for me to get a job after M. Phil in view of my miserable family condition and I am looking to the HOD for this also.

A friend of mine, Sharma, also accompanied SHREEMAAN JI. My friendship with Sharma started with the publication of those two articles on which he wrote some appreciative and critical letters. This exchange of letters befriended us. Sharma is gifted with sharp intelligence and capability. His letters have always been my intellectual feed. Sharma never mentioned SHREEMAAN JI in his letters. He did inform me about his registration for Ph. D. He often mentions his personal economic worries in his letters. Since he was born in a poor family, economic worries followed him from the very beginning. He had to bear the whole burden with father no more. I would console him. I understood his situation because I was also passing through similar situation. We would share each other's sorrow. This alone was the basis of our friendship. When he informed me about his accompanying SHREEMAAN JI in his last letter, I was happy and surprised also.

Sharma recognized me at first sight. He met me with great joy. After some surprise, we threw away all the formalities of our maiden meeting and came out of the department for a cup of tea like everyday friends. There was another reason for this tea. I didn't want to see SHREEMAAN JI as yet and he was busy talking with the HOD and I choose to meet the scholars invited from outside a bit late. The only reason for this habit was that after freeing himself from all formalities and necessary exchange, the HOD should introduce me to him as a brilliant promising student. Sometime is needed to prove the urgent importance of this task for which I engage the HOD instead of meeting myself the invited scholar. Now this habit is a matter of routine. Now my ego is hurt in introducing myself to the scholar visiting the department.

I spent an hour with Sharma while talking over tea. While conversing, I learnt that Sharma was doing Ph. D under the guidance of SHREEMAAN JI. It is on his recommendation that he is working in a press to pull himself on. Today he has come to prepare the press coverage of the lecture of SHREEMAAN JI and meet me.

When I reached the office of the HOD with Sharma, SHREEMAAN JI didn't cast queer glance at me. I got it that all that I desired has happened. Now I was impatient to hear the honey-dipped sentence from the mouth of SHREEMAAN JI – "I have read your articles and have been deeply impressed". This heart's desire of mine was also fulfilled after a few moments. But where other scholars had left the impression of their scholarship by revealing the inner contradictions in my articles making some valuable suggestions, SHREEMAAN JI did nothing of the sort. After speaking that honey-dipped sentence for me, SHREEMAAN JI turned to the discussion that had been going on before our entrance. I started enjoying the discussion of these giants. SHREMAAN JIS's command of the language impressed me. His language had the rising and falling continuous musical flow of a stream which enchanted the listeners. The discussion of the giants couldn't last for a long time because SHREEMAAN JI felt hungry at the invasion of the questions. So that was the end of the discussion.

At lunch-break, Sharma and our HOD were lost in their own conversation and other professors in lunch after talking something with SHREEMAAN JI. Taking it as a good opportunity, I began throwing questions I had prepared after two-three days' labor at SHREEMAAN JI. My joy knew no bounds when SHREEMAAN JI began to pat me on my back and trying to escape by repeating the relevant context. It satisfied and calmed my mind and ego at the success of my labor. Then I hurled an ordinary question at him about Marxist thought instead of asking questions about his own writings. In reply to a question – Who is your favorite writer? – he said in extreme simplicity and innocence, "Nirmal Verma!"

It stunned me for a while. I felt as if I had heard wrongly. I had a desire to ask again. But fearing that that may be true what I had heard. It was impossible to think that a purely personal story-teller like Nirmal Verma can be the favorite writer of a Marxist critic. I felt that I should enjoy the confusion by asking for the Marxist interpretation of Nirmal Verma from

SHREEMAAN JI. But my egoistic mind was not ready to have the honor of being the humble disciple of SHREEMAAN JI by alerting him to his favorite association. I had just thought of ending the context of conversation there that SHREEMAAN JI, unaware of his association, began to enquire about my family condition to continue the chat further. It is a bit difficult for me to talk freely about my economic misery and pitiable family condition with an unfamiliar person. Even then I didn't try to hide any truth. Having some information about my family condition, SHREEMAAN JI expressed some sympathy for me. He advised a brilliant student in me not to be despaired. Then after some futile talk, he expressed his wish to guide me in my research under his care. Thus SHREEMAAN JI finished his lunch with the assurance of helping me in every way.

The auditorium was packed to capacity. In this overcrowded hall, there were bound to listen to this enlightened lecture – professors, the pitiable people like the invited guests to repay their obligations to these professors by relaxing themselves from their boredom with their yawns and forced clappings, the engaged busy students to please these professors and organizers, paid correspondents of the newspapers and also included among them were intelligent people seeking sympathy for their interests in uninteresting and low-level subjects of Hindi Literature.

Whatever our HOD might have been teaching in the class, he has the expertise to drag it into the Indian Culture and teach it; while introducing the Marxist view of SHREEMAAN JI, he used the same technique. While proving the close relationship of Marxist ideology with Indian Culture and with India in the end, he mentioned the unforgettable contribution of SHREEMAAN JI to Hindi Literature and then said all about his greatness I had given him in writing. He never forgets to use my language as his own in this exercise. He invited SHREEMAAN JI to highlight his views on the present status of Hindi novel after saying something more informal.

SHREEMAAN JI started his tale of being a Marxist in the flow of his language after saying something formal about our department and the HOD. After a long introduction, he began to introduce the origin and growth of Hindi novel for the benefit of the students. Sharma was sitting adjacent to me with his pen and paper waiting to note down without losing a moment a beautiful sentence, if any, of SHREEMAAN JI. After giving a detailed introduction to the growth of the Hindi novel, SHREEMAAN JI came down heavily on Hindi Critics for their greater reliance on Western critics instead of referring to the Hindi novels. This tendency has grown so well that sometimes that the criticism of a Hindi novel appears to that of a western critic. This infectious disease is spreading day by day. This is a sign of the mental slavery of Hindi critics. This is the urgent timely need to rid ourselves of this dwarfishness. After this continuous heavy rain on the Hindi critics, he began to discuss the status of Hindi novel in the context of Western novels. SHREEMAAN Ji began to throw light on the personal life of the Hindi novelists and the disgraceful fall of their character after making shallow references to famous Western litterateurs like Dostoevsky, D. H. Lawrence, Kafka, Camus, Sartre etc. how shameful it is that Upendernath Ashak, married thrice whereas Agaya, Dharamvir Bharati, Mohan Rakesh etc. married twice. Ashak wrote his novels on his wives and others on their beloveds. Ramesh Bakashi has not been able to get over the faithlessness of his beloveds. After his love-affair with Mamta, Ravinder Kalia is settled in family life. After describing in detail the love-escapades of Rajender Yadav and Mannu bhandari and many other litterateurs, he began to speak about the impact of their love affairs on their job and society. While talking about the issue of job, he criticized the the novel *Raag Darbari* of Shrilal Shukla. While talking about the corruption in government jobs, he started expressing himself about the totally corrupt face of the present politics, complete loss of values among the politicians and their blind selfishness etc. comparing the Indian politics with the western politics,

SHREEMAAN JI expressed his worry about the increasing influence of the west on Indian cinema. Many writers have also not been able to escape these evil tendencies. Coming down heavily on the influence of cinema on Manohar Shyam Joshi, SHREEMAAN JI showed his deep concern for the fast increasing violence and nakedness in Indian cinema. How can we expect significant and valuable creation of literature in view if this dismal fall in the character of Hindi writers? After these important declarations, saying 'even then', SHREEMAAN JI finished his one-hour lecture giving a general introduction to such Hindi novels on which much has already been written and said.

After the conclusion of the program, the listeners without understanding what SHREEMAAN JI had said in his flow of his decent and cultured language, came out of the hall with their inferiority complex; and SHREEMAAN JI was surrounded by our university students. I stopped a little far away with my friend. As our eyes met, we burst into laughter.

"How will you prepare the report?" I asked.

"As I do usually!"

"You know that I have received the proposal of doing Ph. D?" I informed him.

"It would have been a surprise, if I had not come."

"What do you mean?"

"I mean when a brilliant student like you will work under his guidance, he will teach his classes also, evaluate his answer-books also and….."Sharma paused at this with a straight face.

"And? "

"And also write a book for him as I do."

"I can't believe, yaar!" I said astonished.

"Accept his proposal and see for yourself."

"If it is so, why should the scholars work under his guidance?"

"Dear friend, you can't escape exploitation. You will have to buy daily needs for someone and you will have to drop and collect someone's children from school. Articles have also to be written for them. It's great advantage is that SHREEMAAN JI, being politically well-connected, happy with you, will get you a job also."

"Is he happy with you?"

"Only my newly-written book for him will speak." Sharma felt sad on saying this. Comforting him, I said, "Leave it, yaar. This system is hellish." Then I asked in a lighter tone," the number of research-scholars under SHREEMAAN JI is larger of boys or girls?"

Sharma looked at me with a smile and said," Larger number is of girls. With one or two exceptions, it is not as you think. Girls suit him more for his campaign of writing books. You know girls from poor families looking for livelihood cannot think of revolting. They forget all after getting job with the blessings of SHREEMAAN JI."

"Of course, the real problem is to get a job. It can compel you to accept and do everything."

"That is true."

After a formal good-bye, SHREEMAAN JI came to me while walking with the HOD and other professors. I was engaged with Sharma in my conversation at a distance from these people. Sharma joined the flock of the HOD when SHREEMAAN JI joined me. SHREEMAAN JI patted me on my back, then with his hand on my shoulder, he asked-

"So you are coming? Think carefully before taking any decision. In view of the hint you have given me about your family condition, my suggestion to you is to look for means of earning as soon as possible. You know it well how difficult it is to earn your livelihood. The number of the unemployed is also rising day by day. As a result, it has become difficult to be successful in the competition. This is impossible without any letter of recommendation from an important person and huge amount of money. As such, you will have to face many difficulties. Your brilliance and ability will be caught up in this all. If you think that my views are useful, come to me. Only yesterday, one of the professors of my department has proceeded abroad on one-month study leave. I shall try to get you appointed against a vacant position. Who knows when will a person gone abroad return? Even if he returns, I shall manage a job for you elsewhere. Will get you a research scholarship also. It is not at all difficult for a hard working and brilliant young man like to do research work at our place. You know it well that our city is known as a city of litterateurs. You will have many opportunities for the over-all development of your capabilities. I can do only this much, rest lies on your own will."

SHREEMAANJI reached his car while talking. Before sitting in the car, he again greeted the HOD and others, patted my back and sat in the car. The driver was about to start the car. Sharma open the front door of the car and looked at me. His eyes could see that SHREEMAAN JI had thrown a one to the dog. He cast a sad and sympathetic look at me and sat in the car with a waving of hand.

I don't know why I felt that that waving hand in the air was not of Sharma but of mine.

❖❖❖

8
Dead to all Shame – The Shameless

Shyamlal knew it well that people talk of him at his back as a cheat, clever, cunning, selfish and God knows what else. This disturbed him in the beginning but then he started ignoring them because he had found that everybody here was like that only. He had known everyone as such. He also thought how he could be a clerk in the university if he was so. Can anybody employ such a bad person? This is true that Shyamlal had to do a lot of grinding at many places for many persons – pleading his lies like poverty, family, one-time meal for many days, becoming a sycophant, doing odd job at the place of his Office Superintendent, even offering some money to some – it was only after a hard time that he got a job. Shyamlal had somehow learnt the art of moving on with the borrowings from fellow clerks and friends. Shyamlal knew that he was deep in debt but he had nothing to worry about it, not even regret. Shyamlal had won over everyone with his sweet tongue and tactful lies.

Shyamlal would often think that whatever has done so far, he has done for his family only. who doesn't do so? He did for the education of his children beyond his means. The whole world does so. The whole world is busy looting one another, he is also a part of this world. Then why should he alone be dubbed as a cheat – not the whole world?

This is true that these qualities of Shyamlal isolated him from his friends and his fellow clerks would generally avoid him. He found it of no use. This master cheat was not given any such load of work where he may practice his cheating skills. He would return home after finishing his work leisurely and start running here and there to help his daughter who wanted to be a lecturer in a college after doing M. A. and had applied for a recently advertised post and for which interview was awaited any time, in getting a job. The job of his daughter depended completely on his boss and his boss had assured him of appointment on the condition that she must have some published work. This shook Shyamlal for once but his expertise in telling lies prompted Shyamlal to say that his daughter is brilliant by God's blessing and that she has written a book at this age which is being published and that is why he wants her to be in job that may brighten the life of this innocent girl.

But this issue disturbed Shyamlal for about a week. His daughter had never written even two lines – what to speak about a book. If at all she had any quality, it was that her English was good. He felt that he won't be able to manage a job for his daughter. But this truth was not acceptable to him. All those qualities for which he was known were also of no help or use. It was beyond him to think from where to bring a published book for his daughter. One day when Shyamlal was working against his will in his office focused on this, suddenly, Devghat from Max Prakashan appeared before him like a god. It was three months ago that his boss had written a book for his son and it was his responsibility to take it to the publisher and bring the published matter for proof-reading. Shyamlal had forgotten that he had submitted the manuscript to the publisher. Devghar had come with the proof-reading matter. Shyamlal served him not only tea but also something sweet and salty and returned home with that packet taking half-day leave.

Shyamlal did everything from proof-reading to changing the titles of the chapters and the title of the book and spending money on the publication of twenty copies of the book in the name of his daughter to help her; during that time, Shyamlal kept comforting himself with the thought of mother Kakayi who could demand fourteen-year exile for Shri Ram to seek throne for her son, why he can't do this petty work to get a job for her daughter. Now the sweet tongue of Shyamlal had become sweeter with his colleagues in the office and to shed tears remembering his past with his boss had become his routine. Now Shyamlal lay in wait for that time when his daughter was to appear for interview. He himself remained cautious and also cautioned his daughter when he had arranged his daughter's meeting with his boss. It was Shyamlal's firm belief now that God will fully stand by him in getting a job for his daughter who had always passed her examinations in the first division. He put off his boss when he asked him about the proof-reading matter saying with his honeyed-tongue to bring in a day or two.

Shyamlal was successful in achieving the desired results for his daughter's interview. The whole family was in overjoyed and Shyamlal felt as if he had been secured all life's bliss. He thanked God in millions who had stood by him in difficult times. He was overwhelmed with emotion again and again while thanking his boss on phone. His boss expressed his desire to see his daughter's book as he couldn't see it properly being busy with the interview as her book is almost similar to his own subject, Shyamlal put the receiver back saying –"Just coming Sir."

But he didn't either attend his office or met his boss for three days. He spent these three days in securing the appointment letter for his daughter and her joining as a lecturer. After all this was done, he purchased sweets from the bazaar, picked the packet of proofs and reached the home of his boss; he was sure that his boss will forget the book on seeing the proofs, and even if he asked, he had the art of innocently saying" O sir, I forgot it." Shyamlal knew that the secret of printing only twenty books was not easy to be out in this country because all are lost in themselves only. All are madly engaged in this sort of loot. No one feels concerned with anybody. Even if the secret of truth was exposed, Shyamlal was not worried as he knew it well that here all were whisperers, none to say anything openly. Moreover, this issue would have become old. People are in the fair habit of forgetting all and his daughter would be confirmed in her job by then. Otherwise also, he firmly believed that none can harm him so long as God's blessing he enjoys!

❖❖❖

9
Humanity Desensitized

I woke up at five as usual. I looked to my left as always and found that my wife had gone to the bathroom to purify herself for the hypocritical prayers at worship. "How hypocritical" – I said to myself – obviously, I don't have the courage to say this to her face because after having done so once, I have tasted the war-level fight with her for a week. The fact is that every husband is hen-pecked for one or the other reason. If this tendency has increased in a husband like me, there should be nothing surprising. Soon after marriage, I had realized that to be reasonable with a stupid wife was like hitting your head against the wall, unnecessarily inviting a fight. Then you cannot prevail upon a wife who thinks of herself wise after God and whatever prosperity is there at home, it is a fruit of her prayer and worship only. Who will choose to give up one's studies for such an idiot? When she reads a low-quality book like "Tale of a Weekly Fast", even the touch of which gives me a feeling of disgust, I read Sartre at that time and try to understand life in a better way.

Then the bathroom door opened with a bang. My wife with her hair spread on her shoulders came out muttering something which could be some incantation certainly and went straight to the kitchen. Her muttering seemed as if someone was hurling abuses at someone in heart of hearts. Her face was wrapped in the purity of the whole world. My wife could surpass any world famous actress in acting. You can find such actresses in every home in our country. After having bath, she pretends so chaste as if none has ever touched her. She would hug and embrace me so tightly as if she won't be apart from me. When she wakes up in the morning, she acts as if she were a virgin for the last seven births. "What a hypocrite she is!" I smiled at these thoughts of mine. This description seemed to fit in her personality very well. She will be wanting in any other description.

I know well that she will now pray in her place of worship in the kitchen. Our home being small, a poor professor like me couldn't provide her a big home like any rich person for a separate place of worship. This hypocrite has an illusion of a small temple on a slab in the kitchen wherein she has collected a variety of idols. She has the art of pleasing four-five gods and goddesses in a single prayer as a smart beauty on the threshold youth pleases her four-five lovers with a wink. Look at the wisdom of my wife that she has isolated her living god from these ancient gods and goddesses. A space in the drawing room cupboard is reserved for this. This god dwells in that place of worship. She prays at both these places in the morning. As and when I saw that image, she appeared to be more a *bania* than a devotee or an ascetic. Sometimes while looking at these gods and goddesses, I feel that the allegation against men of being naturally polygamous is baseless. Women enjoy polyandry more. The only difference is that whereas we share the bed with the film actresses, neighborhood beauties or the wives of friends, these enjoy the warmth of the bed with these gods and goddesses who are undoubtedly 'He-men' and have the miraculous powers of fulfilling and satisfying all physical passions. Since Ram, Krishan and Shiva have become antiques, they have their eyes fixed on the living ascetics. Their ceaseless passion sometimes provokes me to quit professorship and start the life of a *sadhu sanyasi*. This is the most rewarding profession. The most coveted honors are possible only in this profession even after swimming and diving with these nymphs in the ocean. How sweet of them that we being their husbands are their gods but they confer this status on the *sadhu sanyasis*. Wives are distanced from their husbands only because of this. I had read somewhere that he who is most sexy becomes religious as much. Indian religion is an anti-dote of sexism. This is the situation only of women, is not true. Some men are also a prey to '*mother fixation*'. They keep crying-mother, O mother! Our country is a museum of such ironies. I vent my anger somewhat in my class or share it with my friend Nirmal who is also a voracious reader like me. He has also discarded all orthodox rituals like me. He is an ardent atheist and argumentative like me. He is more fortunate than me only in one way – that he hasn't married. He is bitterly opposed to the institution of marriage. He is not prepared to restrict his freedom even a bit. The dazzle of fair complexion and lovely face murdered me. The friends did their best to save me by convincing me that a beautiful girl is stupid. But I was to drown myself in the ocean of this beauty and I'm drowned. No shells or pearls fell to my hands. Her blind faith has made my life a hell. In the beginning, I tried to persuade her to differentiate between religion and hypocrisy. No miracles happen in life. No heavenly god or goddess or even a sage ever came to your help. Her worships distanced me from her. Of what use is that worship which discriminates between man and man. My wife distanced me from her in prioritizing hypocrisy over religion.

My mind is crowded with such thoughts every morning as I wake up. I frowned at the ceiling of my room and closed my eyes. Shall sleep visit me? College is closed today – I heaved a sigh of relief at this thought. Then I remembered that it was *Dussehra* that day. Today is the special day for my hypocritical wife to perform prayers and worship and it will last longer today. I don't know how people discriminate with days even! There and then, a question rose in mind if the practice of discrimination started from here only. or the practice of discrimination might have come down to the days. I laughed. How great we Indians are – we discriminate with days even. Then why not do so with man? My hypocrite will keep fast today and visit the temple first with the illiterate, rustic and ugly women of the *mohalla*, taste dirty water as the nectar from the Lord's feet, and then buy something from the fair as a good omen (which is often an image of some god) and returning home, the same routine of shouting foul language at the servants, backbiting of the neighborhood women will begin hearing which anyone can claim the women may be anything but they can't be religious. I remember when I was a child, there used to be a sadhu in our city on whom people had so strong a devotion that they would taste the water flowing from his body when he bathed as the nectar from the feet of the Lord. Even today, people not only wash their body in the Ganga at Haridwar but also urinate therein, wash their clothes there and feel blessed after drinking the same water of the sacred Ganga.

I had just taken a turn in the bed to fix attention elsewhere when I heard someone's footsteps approaching. I looked in astonishment – it was servant there with a *dolchi* in hand. Must be going to bring milk?

"Here is Nirmal babu." He said.

Nirmal, at this hour? I became cautious in utter doubt.

"Send him her." I said and the servant left.

It seemed as if Nirmal had been waiting to be called. The same pyjama, unkempt beard, brown complexion! His face was extremely sad. The news which I had already given to myself, was writ large on his sad face. Nirmal sat beside me and said in low voice, "Yaar, mother is no more."

"Very sad! When did this all happen?"

"I woke up at 1.30 at night. I covered her with a sheet. Thereafter when I woke up, she didn't get up in spite of speaking to her again and again. Then I touch her hands- ice-cold! Felt her pulse but it had stopped. It appears any time after 1.30!"

"What now?"

"You tell me. That is why I have come."

"You want to inform some relative?"

"Do I have any?"

"Even then?"

"No. No one to be informed!" Nirmal said firmly.

"Who is with the dead body at this time?"

"Who can be there? Leaving the dead as such, I have come after locking the house."

I looked cautiously around – my wife might not have heard somehow. I asked enquiringly," How shall we carry her to the cremation ground? You don't want anyone to accompany."

"Of course."

"Okay. Arrange some vehicle then. We shall carry her in that only."

"Yes. This alone will be good. Should I call Dr. Verma?' he asked.

"Do invite if you want. We shall be three with his coming. Even then, vehicle will have to be arranged. Then, we shall need shroud for the body, wood and byre also to consign the dead body to flames."

"We shall have shroud when the shop opens. I have ordered the wood. The watchman of the cremation ground has given the byre made of iron."

"It is okay. You inform me after arranging the vehicle."

"All right. I shall come after arranging the shroud and byre."

I shook my head in consent and he left quietly.

After Nirmal was gone, I felt that my mind was in deep sorrow. Earlier the stupidities of my wife were on my nerves and this sad information. People say that the festival day brings joy. Today for me went waste. People will enjoy festivities on burning the effigies of Ravana and Nirmal will cry at consigning the his dead mother's body to flames. It was astonishing to see Nirmal – how he had controlled his emotions. He didn't want to cry before me. Perhaps he had already cried to relieve himself.

Since I am not in the habit of waking up at five – it is my wife who often wakes me and I tried to sleep again. Watching my wife chewing like gum the age-old shlokas that had lost their meaning while moving about here and there, I felt disgusted – the incorrigible hypocrite! When I tried to divert my attention from this everyday mobile tragedy of my life, my mind paused at the thought of Nirmal.

Nirmal had spent most of his life with his mother in utmost lethargy. His father died in when he was a child. Nirmal had no connection whatsoever with any of his relatives. His own hot-headedness and carefree life being among the main reasons, his mother's unbearable blindness in faith was also responsible for that. She was always afraid that somebody may not use any black art on her only son. She was always perturbed on account of her only son. She was cut off from all the women of the locality due to the fear of this black art. All residents of the *mohalla* were sick of the taunts of this old woman and Nirmal's mother felt unhappy with these foes of her only son. Both lived in their own confined world. She would not let Nirmal meet any relative lest someone should feed him with some necromancy to grab their property. And all the property she had was this home only which tells the tale of her lethargy. Of all, I alone used to visit Nirmal's one-room home with unplastered walls. Perhaps I was the only one whom his mother didn't suspect of any black art. It may be due to my respectable distance with her or my humorous nature or perhaps in spite of my being an atheist or against social customs and traditions like Nirmal, I never argued with her. She would often tell the tales of the conspiracies of relatives to kill Nirmal and Nirmal also agreed with some tales. Nirmal usually quarreled with his mother – on the issue of blind belief. It made him unhappy many times. His mother would not take any medicine in illness. She would usually feel good with the blessing or ashes from a sadhu. Nirmal knew that it was no miracle, only the conditioning of his mother. She would not be seriously ill and she she recovered. I used to talk to Nirmal on this issue for hours. I would see and was scared at thought of the future image of my wife in Nirmal's mother because I knew that the path of blind stupid beliefs in religious rituals leads and ends and is lost in the dark caves. Nirmal was unhappy with the cynicism of his mother, I of my wife's! I would sweat at the thought that one day I too will have to live through this hell of my wife.

Nirmal's mother was down with malaria four or five months before and she didn't take any medicine and looked to her recovery in the blessings of sadhus. This weakened her considerably. She had been to the *deras* of many sadhus. She had swallowed the ashes, fatal for the body but religiously sacred. When all was of no use, then she took refuge at the homeopathic treatment of Dr. Verma. Nirmal's mother agreed to this because the doctor was from her caste only. She recovered from malaria but the delayed treatment couldn't root out the illness and she became sick again. The body had become old and had lost the immunity to withstand the weakness caused by the fasts all life and it demanded good diet for immunity. In spite of being a lavish spender living a carefree life, Nirmal was in a position to provide her good diet. But he was helpless before the childish obstinacy of his mother. Her treatment started again. In this process, whatever little work he used to do, he stopped it. He devoted himself to the care of his mother with whom he had frequent fights but loved her from the core of his being. He took loan from his known persons also forgetting his poverty and capacity. Nirmal had never been worldly wise like us as to save something for his future. He might not have ever visited a bank. I was his closest friend and he shared all this with me. Needless to say that I had also helped him financially in his dire need keeping it as a secret from my wife even.

Bang!

This sudden bang broke my flow of thoughts. I looked back – my wife had fully opened the door of the room. Wrapped in saree, my fair-complexioned wife had loosened hair. Her face had the freshness after a bath and was covered with the sanctity of the prayer. She had a *thaali* in her hand with the earthen lamp lighted in it and a bowl with the Ganga water in it she was sprinkling in all the corners of the room. It was this charm of her beauty that I had made a mistake of marrying her. Oh that there were an instrument to know beforehand the inner beauty of these lovely women! Then perhaps all beautiful girls would have remain unmarried. Who would have dared to marry them? This thought brought a smile on my face.

I remember that time of morning one day when she was engaged in her rituals, she seemed to me very beautiful. It roused my feeling of romance and wanted to make an advance. I felt like hugging her hard and kiss her. Though I know that there is nothing delightful in such a feeling about a wife, I said in a soft voice to excite my mood – you are looking really very beautiful. This didn't bring even a fake blush on her face nor there seemed a sense of pride which comes on the face of every normal woman, not there was a twinkle in her eyes not fake anger on the face which we often see on the women's face in such situations. On the contrary, she pulled more the corner of her saree on her face muttering-"Ram, Ram!" it froze me at once. There appeared a life-long wall that day and I was scared. It occurred to me if she happens to recite this at the time of sexual intercourse, what will become of me? Such thinking kept me scary for days and I lost the courage even to touch my wife. One day I had hardly overcome my fear when she lay beside me as a normal woman, I asked a foolish question as an idolized husband from that chaste wife-

"Do I ever appear in your dreams?"

"What a question it is? You are always with me before my eyes." I knew from her reply that I don't appear in her dreams.

"Then who else is there in your dreams?" I asked with a smile.

"No one."

"Liar."

"No. it is true."

"Even your idolized saint doesn't?" it suddenly escaped my mouth.

"Yes, everyday he comes." Then she revealed all the three who appear in her dreams – my idolized saint, Rama and Krishna.

I learnt for the first time that I don't enjoy any space in her heart in spite of being an idol-husband. There are three lords in the temple of her heart – out of which two don't exist on this earth and nothing to worry about them, but the third, the calamitous, is my rival. Only he sleeps and wakes with my wife. Me the deserted, is there only to be named the father of her children and a submissive lord to manage her daily life – but not a husband in any way. I distanced myself more from my wife that day.

I felt disgust while thinking so. I jerked my head. My wife had left this room to move in other rooms. I found it hard to sleep, I got up with a jerk and went to the bath room.

Lost in these thoughts, I had just come to the dining table for my breakfast and even a holiday went waste – had to write some letters and an article – when the servant came with a message-

"Nirmal Babu has come."

"Why is Nirmal coming again and again today?" placing the kettle before me and interrupting her devotional song, my wife said in irritation, "He should think of festival days. Ill-omened!" she resumed her recitation saying this. I was not surprised at the harsh music amidst my wife's singing. This is her natural daily behavior. Scolding a servant, hurl abuses, to be angry at the sweeper while singing and restart singing is natural to her habit. It is not that my wife alone is expert at such religious chores. One can easily such religious activity in all common homes. There is a woman in my neighborhood who sings bhajans on the mike in the temple, that too on the tunes of film songs and as soon as she reaches home, she not only thrashes her daughter but also hurls such filthy abuses on her that her brilliant intellect is matchless. Later I found this great virtue in all women. I told my wife without any delay lest her dialogue should stretch like a rubber-

"His mother is no more."

"Is it? When?"

"Today morning only." Before her tongue could spit out something else, I left saying that I would take my breakfast later. I have changed my habit of interrupting my wife. I know I'm known as hen=pecked. I too didn't oppose it. Although I say nothing openly to her face, I abuse her in my heart of hearts.

Nirmal sat grief-stricken in my room. He said on seeing me," Yaar, I couldn't arrange a vehicle. In fact, a known person met me on the way as I had left you for this purpose and he runs a tea-shop near my home. He would often enquire about mother's health. He asked me about her health as always and I told him. he began to weep and complained that I didn't even inform him as if I were a stranger. He resented on learning about the vehicle. He talked about two-three servants at his shop, and he too is there. So they would carry the dead body – I have come to tell this to you."

"The vehicle would have been convenient. However, tell me when we have to start for the cremation ground?"

"Around 10.30 a.m."

"It is okay. I shall reach your home in another ten-fifteen minutes." I said looking at the wall clock.

"No. you shouldn't come now. Come only at 10.30. I may arrange the shroud and inform Verma Sahib also. I…" before he could say anything more, my wife happened to reach there. She said without any loss of a moment-

"Nirmal, why did you not tell? Are we aliens? How sad it is. You must have been hungry since morning. Sit and eat something."

"No, Bhabhiji, I don't feel hungry."

"How come that you are not hungry? How will you work with an empty stomach? Get up!"

My wife got him up by the arm and guided to the dining table. I too followed like a submissive child. With Nirmal in the chair, my wife served him a hot fried prantha and a cup of tea. Nirmal began to eat slowly and my wife began to chat with him. I also began to take my breakfast hearing the dialogues of my promising wife. Women have perhaps this inborn quality in them that they behave very practically whatever e the situation. The importance of a mother, helplessness before the inevitable death, we should accept it as the Will of God, there is no way except to endure – I don't know how many hackneyed phrases that are registered for such occasions she was uttering. Nirmal was listening silently with a word or two in between. I observe all in silence thinking that my wife was not adept at talking but at acting also. I learnt about her being an actress when she started meditating at the asking of some stupid ascetic. Even in meditation, she well-knew who is doing what and saying what in home. I had a good laugh at such meditation. Annoyed at my laughter, she gave vent to her anger by switching off my tape-recorder playing ghazals that they interfered with her meditation and I must not listen to them. I stopped using tape-recorder as a proof of my being an obedient husband. But I saw that she winks in her closed eyes in peaceful environment, I had a louder laugh. Then she started doing this covering her face with her *chunni* so that I know nothing. I know not why I felt her hiding her ugliness in her chunni. I was dissatisfied and angry with her behavior. I felt pity also for her. How much deception we have wrapped about to cheat ourselves. What fear haunts us that knowingly we wrap ourselves with such deception. Such pretensions irritate me more. How intolerant and egoistic we are while doing so. My Great India is largely inhabited with such unconscious, moody and hypocritical women. My wife is their mere representative.

After finishing his breakfast, Nirmal was getting up when my wife put a fifty-rupee note in his pocket saying," Keep. It shall be helpful to you. Don't hesitate if you need anything." Nirmal was not in a position to refuse. He was wordless. I led him to the outside gate where he began to cry. He seemed to have lost his suppressed control over himself. I didn't check him. He began to lament while crying, "Yaar, I killed my mother. I am responsible for her death. I didn't serve her well. I always quarreled with her. I killed her."

I put my hand on the back of Nirmal to console him and said, "Why do you think like that? You had been taking care of her for the last four-five months ignoring your work. What else could you do? You gave her the best treatment according to your capacity. It is not proper to blame yourself – you can understand better. Take care of yourself." I patted his back. Nirmal wiped tears from his eyes. Overcoming my own emotions, I asked, "You need money?"

"Of course, I need."

"How much?"

"Four or five hundred are likely to be spent."

"Wait." Saying this and praying that my wife were not there, I went in. she was not there. I took out money from my safe and gave it to Nirmal. Nirmal put it into his pocket and said in sad tone," OK. At ten thirty."

"Yes.' I again patted his back. After he was gone, I returned to my room. Seeing me in the room, my wife stood beside me at once. Then she said without any formality, "Nirmal is moving about here. Who is with the dead body of his mother?"

"Nobody."

"What do you mean?"

I mean nobody by the side of the dead."

"You mean he left it alone? *Ram, Ram*! Does anybody ever leave the dead alone? *Ram Ram*!"

I felt like telling her that it matters a least to anyone if one remains alone all life, how painful it is to the people when the body becomes dust after death. What norms we have made. First, the society isolates one and when one dies enduring the suffering of loneliness, then society is worried about the dead being alone. Such concern with the dead body turned into dust pierced me. But it was all useless to tell my wife. Taking control of my bitterness, I said, "What should he do? He has to arrange shroud, wood etc. He came out locking the home."

"What about his relatives?"

"He is not on speaking terms with them for quite some time. He hasn't even informed them."

"There are people in the Mohall."

"He has been at war with them also."

"In spite of all this, who leaves the dead body alone? Ram, Ram! How ill-omened he is! Leave it, what to us? He who sows, shall reap." My wife said making a face and left the room. Then I heaved a sigh of relief. I was afraid that she might not forbid me to go to Nirmal's house. But my wife didn't do so, though willing, because she knew that though I was hen-pecked, her command won't work here.

My mind was in deep grief. I was not in a mood to do anything. That fair of Dussehra had already been offered to Nirmal. I sat in the bed with my head against the pillow and began to understand this hoax of life.

Nirmal had asked me to reach his home at 10.30. I got ready to reach in time and started on foot. His home was not that far that one couldn't go on foot. This facility is invariably available in a small city.

I noticed a great hustle and bustle on the roads as I came out. All shops on the way were well decorated. Sweet shops were unusually crowded. People from the surrounding villages also come here on their tractors on this day. This adds to the hustle of the city. So special police arrangement are made to control and regulate the crowds. The routes for the movement of traffic are also fixed. Presently this arrangement had not been made for it was the morning time.

There is a huge crowd across the eastern part when you cross the G. T. Road, because two cinema halls are also situated there in that bazaar. Nirmal's home is also in the street on the left on this very road. Enjoying the hustle of the market, I reached the corner of the street. I resumed my sadness as I entered the street. I stood before Nirmal's one-room home with a *kachcha* arena. His locked door baffled me. What to do now? That door could have been easily opened with a little forced push as its wood was too old to stand. The brick-walls had never been cemented. I knew well the nature of Nirmal that he would love to spend on books than on cementing the walls. Nirmal's reading habit was almost a mad craze. He had spent all his life's earnings on books. His mother felt so sick of his reading habit that she got disconnected the electricity-supply. She herself lived in darkness so that the light of her son's eyes stays.

I came out of my reflective mood and had turned to walk when I saw Nirmal coming on his cycle. He stopped near me and gave me the key to unlock the door saying," You go in, I shall come with Verma Sahib. I shall ask Vijay also to come with his servants. "

He turned his cycle and left before I could say a word. I opened the lock and went in and bolted the door otherwise it opens again. On the door's left was *kachcha* compound with a tap water with a brick wall around to create the illusion of a bath room. On the right side were two rooms – the first was kitchen-cum store for all provisions. The second was an all-purpose room with two cots, a box and a very big sheet box and all the alcoves in the room were full with books. The room was wholly damp as its roof was also *kachcha.* I was shaken when I reached the door of the room. Nirmal's mother, dead and covered in white sheet, was lying the charpoy there. I entered there with hushed steps. Was seeing some dead body. It was a queer wait that there might be a movement in the body. My face shone with a drop of perspiration at this thought. There and then, a thought came what if my wife comes now. " Hay Ram, the dead body has not been brought down on the floor since night. Shiva, Shiva!" There can be other reaction of hers than this dialogue. I don't know why the sight of the dead body in the charpoy didn't annoy me. It is not possible that it didn't occur to Nirmal to place the dead body on the floor. He was alone and he was not in a position to call someone for help. But it hardly matters. I don't know why I took Nirmal's mother's dead body lying in the charpoy a symbol of Nirmal's sensitive attachment with his mother whereas I have seen people placing the body of their dearest dead on the floor. This process is essentially associated with loss of love and separation.

I felt suffocated in that room. I felt like going out but there was sharp sunshine which I couldn't bear. I had to stay in that very room. That dead body had been provoking a variety of thoughts. I found that in spite of being an intellectual, certain strange fears which have no basis reside in me. Childhood fears, stories of ghosts and spirits and horror movies lie deep in my unconscious. The dead body lay unmoving and there was not even a remote possibility of a miracle but what to do with the fear that was a part of my *sanskar*. The thought that one day I shall also be like – unmoving and frozen – was disturbing me. This fear began to sting me again and again. In an attempt to avoid the sight of the dead body, I continued looking at it.

I wanted to liberate myself from my thinking and the strange habit of continuously looking at the dead body. I picked the book from the top of the heap of books lying on that big sheet box. Dusting off its title cover, I found that it was Saul Bellow's novel *Herzog*. I remembered somewhere written in this novel that one couldn't love a religious woman. Earlier I took this idea of Saul Bellow as a concoction but I know now that such concoctions are also experienced truths. Such women ignoring their husbands keep enjoying the *Prasad* from a variety of *sadhu*s and also delight in the fruit somewhere. In the olden times, this practice was *niyoga*. Today, this is called the blessing of God,, blessing of the saint or the fruit. In the olden days also, women were impregnated by feeding them with kheer (rice, sugar and dry fruit boiled in milk till hardened) or fruit and it is so even today. A devotee may or may not understand its meaning. My wife too would have done the same if I had not given her the fruit in disturbed mind. Even then, she didn't stop following the sadhus. Only God knows how many apples and bananas she ate to be blessed with a son. She went up to Haridwar in this pursuit. The home was flooded with the pictures of gods and goddesses. I started having horrible dreams at the sight of these pictures. What the poor scientists cannot do, my wife tried to do that through the apples and bananas of sadhus and the lifeless pictures of the gods and goddesses. Always a single prayer to God! I would also laugh to think at what task these foolish women have engaged Him. After all this quackery, my wife was blessed with a daughter. God be thanked that my mother had died otherwise she would not have spared her daughter-in-law for this evil deed. She would have punished her with taunts all her life for the disgusting crime of having borne a daughter. The birth of a daughter didn't diminish the desire of my wife. she took it as the fruit of the *karmas* of the previous birth. I also thought this that let her enjoy the fruit of the karmas of the previous birth when I am not interested in the second child.

I left the book there only and picked the magazine lying on the top of the heap at hand. I found on dusting it that it was *Debonair*. I had given this magazine to Nirmal to read a thought-provoking article published therein. My hand touched straight the middle page that is generally folding. This page shows the naked body of a beautiful woman by covering the front part. The sight this 'centre spread 'page often gives me the feeling how soon the wives lose their charm. Such realization becomes deeper when they bear a child. That gives the husband a second rank. If the wife happens to be religious, the husband is at the lowest rank.

God knows whom this beautiful woman with a yellow cloth on her thighs in the half-lying posture was watching. This yellow cloth was not meant to hide the obscenity of her body because a naked body with all the organs is not obscene, it has sanctity. I don't know why I took this yellow cloth as a symbol of Indian censorship for which the body may be seen as vulgar but the shallow kissing and embracing in film songs is not obscene. I was lost in the body of that beautiful girl – this picture was an anti-dote in the suffocation of that room. At that very time, there was a knock at the door. I closed the magazine at once and jumped to the door with an eye of the dead body in white sheet.

There was not Nirmal as I opened the door but a fat man with pots of milk and ghee in his hands in dirty clothes with three men stood there. He became a little hesitant seeing a stranger in home and said, "Where is Nirmal?"

"He is just coming, has gone to bring his friend." Saying this, I moved to another side of the door. All those four came in. a woman was also there with them. She remained outside and began talking to a woman standing before her. I recognized that fat man as Vijay only. The face of some people reveals their profession. Vijay also looked to be a milk-vendor and tea-shop owner. His three men leaned against the outer wall of the room and began smoking *bidis*. When

Vijay came before the main room, his eyes fell on the dead on the charpoy. "The dead body has not been taken down....well, do this work." Vijay spoke as if to himself. I pretended to move but those three put out their bidis and stood up. They took down the dead body along with the bedding and placed it on the floor. The iron-pipe bier lays outside the room. Leaving it on the ground, Vijay said to himself, "I don't know whether he has brought ropes or not."

Some women from the Mohall had taken three-four rounds from outside since the door was open. Perhaps they wanted to come in but the presence of the strangers inside prevented them. They all began talking with Vijay's wife.

At that very time, Nirmal's cycle stopped in front of the door. Dr. Verma was also seen on his scooter. Nirmal brought in his cycle and Verma Saheb his scooter. Both came and stood by my side. Then Vijay's wife came to Nirmal and said, "Sunny, the ladies are ready to accompany you to the cremation ground. You just ask them once."

"No, I won't." Nirmal said firmly, "Those with whom I had no connection all my life, now I won't fold my hands before them. It doesn't matter if they don't go."

"Very right. This is not the time for feminine grace. They should have been ready without any formal asking."

That lady seemed despaired with these words of Verma Saheb. I being pro-wife now, I liked compromise that I was going to suggest to Nirmal to let those women accompany us but I chose to be silent on seeing the firmness on Nirmal's face after what Verma Saheb had said.

"Is the dead body not to be given an obsequious bath?" Nirmal beckoned to Vijay's grieved wife.

"I cannot do this, Doctors have forbidden me to bend. There is a problem in my backbone. He knows it." She said pointing to her husband. Vijay shook his head in agreement and I understood that he is also helpless before his wife.

"If it is so, we won't give her a bath. Of what use will the bath be." Nirmal said in firm voice. He went in the room and came out with a plastic bag. Taking out the stitched shroud, he said," We can cover her with it as we can't put it on her."

Vijay's wife went out with her head hanging. I and Verma Saheb stood alone. Whatever had happened and what was going to happen, God knows how she would have taken it if my wife had seen this all. She would have pounced heavily on them all and allowed the body to be carried after performing all religious rites. These rites are all foolish for Nirmal and myself, even Verma Saheb didn't seem religious to me.

Those three persons put the dead body on the bier on receiving a hint from Vijay. Vijay was unhappy with these happenings as was evident from his face. He was like a real brother of my wife. He felt helpless only. Suddenly the feelings of respect and jealousy rose then in my mind. Nirmal was free.

He could do whatever he liked and was doing whereas I would have done all even unwillingly.

After placing the dead on the bier, the shroud was put on it. Nirmal gave the rope and they all began to tighten the dead with the bier. I was also going to join this exercise when Nirmal made me get up with his hand on my shoulder and took me to the head of his mother saying, "Yaar, my mother treated you after me as her own. Before we move with dead to the crematorium, I wish that you place your hand on her forehead."

I looked at Nirmal and saw him in tears. Nirmal was right in saying. Really she looked upon me as equal to Nirmal and wished me to take care of him after her. My mother had died long back – and I found the same attachment with Nirmal's handicapped mother after long.

I bent down, removed the shroud from her face and placed my hand on her forehead. The forehead was cold. Leaving my hand there for a moment or two, I removed my hand and covered the face again. I found Nirmal crying. Verma Sahbe consoled him. I also tried to control my emotions. My wife would never have let me do this. Had I done so freeing myself from her terror, she would have washed my hands in the Ganga water and sought the forgiveness her gods and goddesses for my sins.

Nirmal and Vijay were at the head of the bier and the two fellows at the rear. A half-dead person picked the small pots of milk and ghee. I locked the house and came out. The ladies of the mohalla were enjoying the scene with Vijay's wife. Verma Saheb set out with me.

The bazaar presented the same hustle I had seen earlier as we took the turn from the street. People were watching the funeral and were astonished to see only two men following the funeral. Although the distance between Nirmal's house and the G. T. Road was hardly five hundred meters, the bearers of the bier changed their places twice – those on the right came to the left and vice versa. Then I realized the heaviness of the bier. The iron pipe hurt the shoulder. All the four began to feel breathless while reaching the G. T. Road. Their back was drenched in perspiration. That half-dead man handed the pots to me to be in his master's place to free him. Vijay wiped his neck with the hanky to walk beside me. I asked-

"Is it heavy?"

"Yes, it is quite heavy."

"It is made of iron pipes. That is why. I had asked Nirmal to arrange a vehicle."

"Yes. It would have been okay the. It was I who had advised him against this. What did I know that this would be like this. What can be done now? It will have to be borne now." Saying this, Vijay asked Verma Saheb to be in Niraml's place and himself replaced his own man. That man and Nirmal kept walking beside me for some time. Then Nirmal replaced another bearer. We were passing through the Books Market after crossing G. T. Road. Crowd here was larger for the road was narrow. People looked happy. I would often visit this market. All knew me. I was feeling good in the image of my being a professor. Following the bier with the pots of milk and ghee had endangered my image. So I wanted that we should quickly pass through the market. I had no feeling of being alone behind the bier and it was here that that corpse of a man had disappeared freeing himself. Some thought brought a smile on my lips. At the same time, the thought of being a bearer drenched me in perspiration. When I looked at the bier in front, I was relieved that I was quite short-statured and they wouldn't imbalance it. The low feeling of being short-statured turned to real for the first time.

All the five were relieving one another and while we were passing by the temple after the market when Vijay following asked Nirmal ahead –

"We are not to stop at gurudwara or temple?" he was asking as if he wanted some rest for all.

"Nowhere to stop, yaar? You know well that I am a non-believer."

"Let us stop for some time." Vijay couldn't help saying.

"Of course. We shall stop there." Said Nirmal.

Away from the temple is an empty space where the sweepers dump the garbage of the town. At the end of that, the bier was brought down there and place aside. The condition of the five was pitiable – perspiring, gasping for breath, they stood around the bier. Vijay's companions were surely cursing him. They would run away leaving the dead there if it were up to them. I asked Nirmal-

"Is it heavy?"

"Yes."

"I told you to hire a vehicle. There would have been no trouble."

"That would have been better." Said Verma Saheb.

Nirmal kept silent. His silence and sadness were understandable.

They lifted the bier again after ten minute rest. Seeing the bier on the roadside near the heap of garbage, the passersby were shaken – all of them were the brethren of my wife, but none of them took their note. All felt tired. It was a compulsion to move on. The path was straight. The way to the crematorium starts here. All were in a hurry to be free from this burden on reaching the burial ground.

They reached there at last. All the faces were showing the signs of tiredness and relief. I was happy inside as I didn't have to carry the bier. It was at least good that telling this to my wife, I could win her praise.

The watchman of the ground for the dead fixed the iron rods in the corners of the space for the dead to be consigned to flames where the logs of wood were kept. Then all joined hands to place the bier there. The logs were properly placed then and the trash was pushed below. Nirmal stood there lost in himself. Suddenly, he went to the watchman and asked, " I know nothing what to do. You tell me what I have to do.? These people have brought milk and ghee."

"This is a matter of your faith, Sir. I can call pundit if you say."

"No. Pundit is not needed."

"It hardly matters. You pour milk and ghee around the dead on the pyre and also pour ghee on the dead. That's all." Nirmal did as he was told. First milk, then ghee he poured. Without doubt, Vijay had brought this. After all, he believed in such rites. Nirmal was tense otherwise he understood the sense of belonging. This alone was his value. So he raised no objection to all this.

Nirmal consigned the dead body to flames. The pyre was in flames. We were watching the flames rising. Nirmal was crying. When the flames were high, the watchman gave Nirmal a stick to be pressed the hollow space at the head of the pyre. With the low cracking sound, we all retreated with Nirmal.

"Now you all go. I shall sit here for some time." Nirmal's tone was wet. I and Verma Saheb beckoned Vijay and his men to leave. Wiping his face, Vijay picked the pots and left with his men. I sat with Nirmal and Verma Saheb on the nearby cement bench.

Nirmal began to cry loudly at the sight of the flames rising from the pyre. He was completely broken inside. Verma Saheb was also in tears. I too would have been deeply touched like them but I overcame myself. Nirmal again began to lament, "I killed my mother. I didn't look after her properly. I kept quarrelling with her all my life. I didn't give her proper medical treatment in her illness. Verma Saheb, I doubted you also that you were giving her indigenous medicines, not made in Germany." Normal kept weeping repeating this. Verma Saheb wiped his tears and began patting his back with me.

All of a sudden, Nirmal got up and ran to the fire. We could at once guess the tragic happening and ran after him. We held him back. he began crying there-"Let me die. Leave me. I have no right to live. I killed my mother." We brought him back to the same bench with difficulty. He kept sobbing there. He repeated himself a little later. We were cautious this time. We held him by the arm and made him sit there. I said-

"what are you doing, Nirmal? You are a wise man. It is not expected of you. What will come of suicide?'

"Let us go from here." Verma Saheb said.

"You leave. I shall sit her for now."

Verma Saheb and myself looked at each other. We took a silent decision that Nirmal was not to be left there alone in any condition. He can do anything nasty. We engaged ourselves in meaningless talk to diver Nitmal's attention. Nirmal started crying again while talking. He asked us five-six times to leave as he didn't wanted to be there. He repeated his earlier attempt twice again.

This disturbed balance of Nirmal was new as well as shocking for me. I had always found him an intellectual who had no space for emotions. I had seen him living as such also. He is an unbeatably argumentative. Whatever touch of emotion I had seen him, it was only when he talked about his mother. It was so because he lived with his mother. Who else was there for him except his mother? I thought in my folly that he would respond to his mother's death as an intellectual only. but I had forgotten that he too was a human with a heart in his bosom that always beats and which has not yet turned into a stone. Sometimes, a man wears the garb of intellectuality to hide his extreme sensitivity from the sharp poisonous nails of the world. I didn't think of Nirmal as such. These actions of Nirmal may seem to be his momentary emotions to some but his this human character impressed me a lot.

Nothing rational could be discussed with Nirmal today because he would have cut it with the sword of his emotionality. So myself and Verma Saheb kept talking to him emotionally for about two hours. Nirmal was not ready to get up from there. The stream of emotions suppressed under years of intellectuality had begun to flow unstoppably. Even then we succeeded in persuading him to come out of the cremation ground. The three of us lost in talking stopped before Nirmal's home. I unlocked the door. Verma Saheb brought out his scooter.

We both didn't go in. I did so intentionally. I knew that this empty home will rouse greater emotions in Nirmal. I again locked the door after Verma Saheb had left. Before leaving, Verma Saheb not only prevailed upon Nirmal but also invited him to his home.

I was feeling hungry and Nirmal had carried the iron pipe bier. So I felt that he too would be hungry. We came out of the street and turned to the left. There was Vijay's shop in front of Adarsh Cinema. Cinema was very near. Vijay not only made us sit in but also sent tea and some saltish. I wanted to invite Nirmal to tea and lunch and talk to him. Nirmal was also hungry. It was clear from the way he was taking tea and eating the saltish but there was someone in him that was killing his hunger – you may call it the flow of emotions without doubt.

Nirmal again showed his obstinacy to go to the cremation ground while taking tea. I asked him to bring him round-

"What is there now, Nirmal?"

"Mother is there."

"No, mother is not there. Only ashes are there – burning ashes."

"Even then I have to go there."

It was a fresh trouble for me. I was alone also. I was quite short statured beside him. I alone couldn't stop him. even then, I engaged him in talking and suggested that we should keep loitering the rest of the day. He agreed and came down on the road with me.

Discussing life and literature with Nirmal gives the joy of a literary debate. I was not at all in a mood to be argumentative because sitting alone by the dead body of his mother since morning and then staying in the burial ground for such a long time had left me with a strange feeling and there was heaviness in the head overpowered by sadness. But something had to be done. I knew that he too was badly shaken today. That interruption shall be missing from his chat. After talking in this way, I started telling him about his life to come. I convinced him that his life would be totally different from now. He will have to reshape his thinking. His problems would now be from food to emotionality. God knows how much I spoke to Nirmal in this way. He kept listening to me. Sometimes he would interrupt saying, "Yaar, I feel like going to the cremation ground." Many times, I would keep silent on listening to him, sometimes ignoring, I would continue and also give him a light dose sometimes. His feeling returned to the surface time and again. It seemed natural to me.

The town was bustling with joy heavily till evening. People from the surrounding villages were gathering in the Ram Lila

Ground to enjoy the burning of Ravana's effigies. The wheel-barrows were stuck on both sides. It was not possible to hear one's own voice in the chaotic din. When the crowd became unbearable for us, we both came out. I had been fatigued by now and wanted to go back to my home. The effigies of Ravana had been sent into flames and people had begun returning. Nirmal was my trouble. I knew that it was dangerous to leave him alone in his home. He could do anything. I made up my mind to take him to my home today. I told him then-"Nirmal, you go with me to my home today and stay there."

"As you think proper! " Nirmal responded as if he wanted it. I like his response.

We reached home lost in talking. I led him to my room and went out to inform my wife. She was seen coming from front with her head covered with her chunni. She seemed to have returned from the temple after offering prayers. Her face looked peaceful after incantations.

"Listen, Nirmal will stay here only today. I have brought him alive with great difficulty."

"What?" said my wife interrupting her incantations, "You have brought that ill-omened home? Ram, Ram! Think at least of the auspicious days. What should I do if his mother is dead? Am I bound to take care of him? Today you have brought him on the auspicious day. Fuck him off from here – otherwise I shall be at my worst, you understand?" my wife was shouting and I was seeing her peaceful face in recitation of incantations or the flames of anger rising on her calm face and at the same time, she carrying a *thaal* decorated with the sacred Ganga water and other articles of prayerful worship and an earthen lamp burning with a carefree expression of indifference!

❖❖❖

10
The Denied, The Deprived and The Destitute

He felt tired while moving restlessly in his room and sat in the chair. He was unable to understand what to do. He had a heap of questions in his head to which he had no satisfactory answer. He couldn't understand for which fault of his he had been thrown out so humiliatingly. He had an equal share in that one-crore home, fifty-lakh shop and fifty-lakh factory. But his flexible temperament and his lack of supine had transferred the whole property in the name of his elder brother and his wife under their influence and he had been ordered to leave home. When he called his married sisters to protest against this injustice with him, those *kaliyugi* sisters thinking that this unmarried school master will not be able to perform all the ceremonies on behalf of the maternal family at the time of the marriage of their daughters and worried about the same, they also stood by the elder brother. So he was left in the lurch with all his ideals, principles, honesty and his orthodox view of the relationships. He had tasted the naked disgusting truth of life for the first time and when he left home with the boxes packed with his books, his father or his brother and his wife had not gifted him even a piece of torn and dirty cloth to clean them, what to talk of a broken old pot or utensil.

Whatever is there today in this rented room is given out of pity for this gentleman master by the landlord and the poor helpless was burdened with gratitude. Uneasiness and tensions have been killing him since he has shifted to this place. Schools are closed for summer vacation and he lies the whole day in the charpoy sad and perturbed about this cursed life feeling embittered and irritated thinking that the basis of relationships in this century is not belonging and love but selfish interests and greed for money.

He had gone to his father's shop with the boxes of books paying for his ideals to show his reverence but the father saying "I am helpless", said farewell to his son. So he sat sad, broken and helpless with his boxes and old charpoy given out pity by the landlord in the rented house like an absolute pauper after giving up his claim of share in the one-crore worth kothi, fifty-lakh worth shop and fifty-lakh worth factory. He was lost in reflections if all this had happened if his mother had been alive.

He had his own identity of a studious and scholarly person in the city. None had ever heard him talking in high tone. It was a part of his decent training to respect everyone and treat them nicely. The elder brother might have been notorious for his drunkenness and dirty tongue but he was the first choice of the father. That is why, his father took courage to utter this dialogue "I am helpless." And in utter shock, he kept looking at his face. He had never expected this sentence but when he had got what he had desired? Today his life was on the road after being confined to one room in his own home. All his life, he had shared the warmth of close belonging and relationship with his elder brother, his wife and their children. His sharp and clever, insensitive and good at telling lies brother's wife and beating the cunning film actresses in acting, she had enslaved his brother and father with these qualities. Overlooking all these tactical postures, he laughed them away valuing relationships and his brother and his wife kept planning how to get rid of this undesirable claimant and successor to share in parental wealth. His shallow idealism, stupid thinking of valuing relationships and honesty suffered a severe setback before wealth. As a result, he was now in a small rented room with all his stupidities and vices.

His known felt helpless in their sympathies – his family was bitterly condemned in the town. But this could do no good to him. his friends suggested that suing his father in a court of law was the only right course to which he replied that he needed time to think. Today, his friends had gathered in his room to discuss this issue. He had asked for chairs from the landlord. He was grateful for his generosity and felt disturbed comparing him with his blood relations. Generally his friends would talk for hours on society, country, philosophy, politics etc for hours but now they were all silent as if there was nothing to talk about. He knew that his friends were unhappy with his present condition because his friends are far more honest than his family. When silence became unbearable, one of his friends cleared his throat to initiate the talk-"so" and asked after a pause-

"So what did you decide?"

When he cast a questioning look at his friend, his friend said – "Are yaar, about filing a suit. We all". Pointing to his three friends, his friend said, "They all feel that you must take this step. This is the demand of justice. We have decided about the lawyer also. We need only green signal from you."

"No, dear Vinay, I shall not file a suit."

"You are committing a folly." said his other friend.

"You have as much claim over that property as has your brother."

"And then," said the third friend," you are demanding your right only. You are not encroaching upon anybody's right."

"You are right, Ravi. But you forget that this property belongs to my father. He ha the right to give it to anyone he likes. Then the people will say that the son sued the father for money. Nobody shall understand the grave injustice done to me."

"Let the people go to hell. Let them say whatever they want." Ravi said.

"I had asked him not to leave home, we shall see what they do." said the third friend looking at the other two.

"What else could he do if he had not left home, Ramesh. He was fed up with daily taunts and their ill-treatment. Then when father surrendered, what could I do?" he said in sadder tone.

"That is how it is. Your father... is" Vinay checked himself from being abusive.

"Then there is one thing more." Said he, "The suit will not end early. It may take five to ten years at least. Then if I get a little bit of my share, of what use it would be. Just think of those years of tensions and misery I will have to endure. During this, if something wrong happens to dear father, God forbid me, everybody will blame me." His tone was the same sad. He became intensely serious. He was overwhelmed with emotion. He controlled his emotion and said-

"And the more important than this all about which nobody thinks and which is mentally troubling me is – trust in relationships. I sacrificed this value while leaving home. This value is the basis of life and I have been deprived of this basis. My family doesn't realize that they haven't snatched wealth but my life from me. Wealth has wings. But how can I live by losing whatever I have lost. Now I am left with no values of life, no faith, no trust. I am an orphan now though I have a father, brother and three sisters. There is none in the whole clan who could stand by me and keep up my courage. No one is concerned. They all can indulge in backbiting against them but none has the courage to say anything in their face. Now I realize the power of wealth. The ideals, the values I learnt from the books are dashed to ground. What shall I do with wealth in such a situation? Who will understand my pain, who will feel this harsh truth that I am dead inside." Saying this, he became silent. He was really overwhelmed and his friends noticed tears in his eyes – tears that are shed at the death of somebody!

11
A Tale of an IDIOT

Friends, it is very important to know why a story-teller like me gave this nomenclature to him before I begin to tell his tale. I chose to give him this name because he was a dreamer. You will at once say that all are dreamers – some less, some more – then are we all idiots? As a rule, we are – every dreamer is an idiot here or there because knowing that dreams are not a reality, we all are lost in dreams. What else should I call it-if not idiocy? This character has been delineated only for your recreation. Yes, then, our idiot hero was a dreamer all through. He enjoyed all happiness in life only in dreams. He had devoted himself wholly to dreams – first as a matter of love, then as a habit and then as a compulsion.

Since I am living in the last phase of the 20th century, I agree with Freud's scientific assumption that it is necessary to know the childhood of any person to know and understand him. That is why I also want to begin my tale with the foundation of his dreams he laid in his childhood. If I sit to write all about his childhood, it is possible that it may turn out to be a complete novel for which I have neither time nor courage. Even if I do it, I know it fully well that the readers of this age of hurry and worry or high speed like you will have no time to read it. To be brief, I shall mention only that aspect of his childhood which has direct relation with his beautiful dreams. His family background will have to be essentially introduced before that. It is said that the family environment alone influences most a person. Our hero too is influenced by that. He couldn't be an exception to this.

He was also born and brought up in a middle class family like many other heroes. Sweets had been distributed to celebrate his birth as a male child like many other idiot heroes of India. But he was uniquely different from many other heroes in two ways. Firstly, he fell into the hands of doctors when he was born. He had no light in his eyes. He got some light after five small and sixth big operation so that he could see the ugliness of this world. (This story-teller hasn't used the word beauty since it doesn't exist in this world.) I may explain his weak sight so that there is no space for any illusion left. Our hero had to wear glasses bearing 12-numbered for the whole of his life. Even after putting on these glasses, he had a very limited vision.

He had different 16-numbered glasses for reading purposes. These numbers kept rising with age. There are very few fortunate even among the aged who wear such high-numbered glasses. It is with this weak eye-sight that our hero enters this world. His mother also, God alone knows, in how many temples, offered prayers, made huge offerings, kept fasts but no miracles happened as they happen in Puranas and films. There was no change for the better in her thin slim son. No heavenly god or goddess took pity on him. but his mother didn't give up her hope and kept offering prayers and seeking blessings for her son. It can be controversial if such a hero is called handicapped. I would simply move forward saying that his eye-sight was extremely weak so that I can escape the academic significance of this controversy. There is no such unique character at least in Hindi literature is neither blind nor has vision. (I was going to say the world literature but, in view of my own limitations, I felt compelled to keep myself confined to Hindi Literature only). All this is meant to convey that our hero was born with inferiority-complex.

No hero has been blessed so far with the second uniqueness also. The father of the hero is often a merchant or a shopkeeper or a licentious merry-maker or a poet or a labor. But the father of our hero, though a trader, was not even a trader. His father was a theatre-owner in which were shown the porn movies from Bollywood to Hollywood. I can affirm on the strength of my studies that I haven't read anywhere that the father of the main or the leading character of any creation was the owner of a cinema hall. This uniqueness also fell to the lot of this hero. Here I would like to mention for the satisfaction of the believers of the Principle of Heredity another unique quality that his father, in spite of his being the owner of a cinema hall, was extremely noble and gentle. The owners of the cinema halls are usually bad characters in the same way as the liquor-vend owners. His father committed no other sin to bear him. as a result, the virtue of nobility also fell to the lot of the hero. The nobility of the hero's father was so perfect that he never sold tickets in the black market. Consequently, the family didn't prosper as it should have. Well, the basis of this unique hero's being a dreamer who happened to be the fourth among his brothers and sisters lies in the significance of these two qualities.

This unique hero experienced two unique things – actually only one, his forced situation was the second. The first was his utmost security, his additional care. Mother would not let him be out of sight even for a moment. This excessive security and care alone made him extremely nervous, shy afflicted with inferiority. There was a limit to this security after which the family began to ignore him. that is right too. How long can one provide security? There are five other children also in the family. They too are to be taken care of. He was left all alone to himself after two more children. He was left to himself. What did the parents of ordinary intelligence know or little did they know that this helpless looking, unwanted and weakling child would become an enlightened character of Hindi Literature with the blessing of this story-teller one day.

All the residents of the locality would look at this our hero with profound pity. How weak he is, even at this age, he has to wear so thick glasses! "Hoy, how weak he is! Does she not feed her properly?" he would keep listening to this all. He didn't like it at all from his very core. And he was unable to say this. His mother would take special care of his feed but all her hopes were fixed on her elder son. He alone was the hope and anchor of all. Our hero was himself an invalid – what support he could be for anybody. May he grow up to bear his own burden – this was the only blessing his mother sought! His mother had only one worry – what will become of this child? Who will look after him after she was gone? His mother would think and feel sad – she might have wept also! This is found only in India where a mother showers her love equally on the invalid child as on other healthy ones. Obviously, our hero's mother remained tense because of him because she was a truly Indian mother – full of love, innocence and motherhood. His brothers and sisters had no attachment with him. Even his father had no attachment with him to speak of. He doesn't remember if his father ever chatted with him or lifted him in his lap. His father was a terror for the whole family, including him. he had to often listen from his father-"Stupid!" his father would often scold him because his younger sister who was the most loved in the family especially by his father, would get him beaten with false complaints against him. She would do all wrongs blaming him. The psychiatrists kept looking for the reasons. The hero would see that whenever the mother felt sick of all this, beat him and would herself start crying. He could give no proof of his innocence to his mother. All this made him inward-looking afflicted with inferiority complex and extremely sensitive with nothing but loneliness.

These feelings of inward looking and inferiority were very helpful and which stood with him all his childhood as they were often repeated and his proud father couldn't understand how his far-sighted influence could help him pass B.A. (Hons.) in Philosophy and be a learned scholar.

His father would often invite one or the other of his friends to lunch or dinner. Such event was organized at least once a month. Then he was specially instructed not to join them. Undoubtedly, he was dressed very well but he had to stay in a separate room. He was served his food also there. That innocent child would take his food alone in the adjacent room during the party terrorized by his father. He would listen to the pieces of conversation and laughter of the family members and god knows what thoughts passed in his little brain. When all returned to the drawing room after tasting to the full the delicious food, he would be called there and was requested to sing for them. He would start like a wound toy and entertain with his game. On hearing about the party being thrown at home, all would burst into joy, saddening him alone as an innocent desire to eat with all in the party woke up in him and which remained unfulfilled. There was none among all his brothers and sisters with whom he had a feeling of attachment. There was nobody in the family who would try to understand his mindset and show him love and boost his morale or even revolt against the injustice being done to him. The most painful for him would be that even his younger sister joined the party. He was kept out of the party, though he was elderly to her. He was an unwanted person for all who could be rebuked or scolded or then used for entertainment. When his elder brother also invited his friends to dinner, he too would use his father's technique of inviting our innocent hero to "after-dinner entertainment". All this show continued! Our hero came to believe sooner or later that he was not deserving of more than that, he is an idiot perhaps, he doesn't know the table etiquettes perhaps to sit and eat with all. He shrank himself with such thoughts that his self-confidence remained confined to reciting happy songs. He sang sad songs only on the roof. He could never understand why he was treated like that. He was neither naughty nor obstinate. Now who would make him understand that only he who is an idiot is treated like that in this world. He was the same in his family. Otherwise also, he was a burden on the family. His parents couldn't kill him, he was alive only then. Ugly things are always negligible and treated as such. He learnt this all quite later whereas he was a child then, like other children,, who was helpless in a compelling situation to pass through such unusual unhappy experiences.

It would have been better if it had stopped there. But his family didn't stop there. Whenever there was a general discussion on any problem in the family, if he gave his opinion with all, he was reproached without any thought saying, "You keep quiet, you know nothing, don't interrupt." He would be quiet then. Sometimes he would be asked to leave the place. He would then leave quietly. If they were to go to join a party, he was told, "what will you do there, stay at home." By and by, he not only stopped interfering in the family matters but also stopped going anywhere. All foolish decisions the family took all life and endured resultant sufferings, that "IDIOT" was not to be blamed even remotely for that. Knowing well the consequences of those wrong decisions, he couldn't save his family.

Our hero couldn't attend parties or marriages or other social get-togethers with an open mind. Wherever he went, he remained uneasy. Nobody ever tried to understand this uneasiness behind the tragedy of that "IDIOT". Behind this inferiority and loneliness in him is the negligence he had to suffer in his family from his childhood till the last moments of his life.

Cinema hall used to be his best attraction. He felt like sitting there all the time. He would remember the film scenes and they would keep lingering before his eyes. He sang film songs but he liked only those songs which were sad in tone singing of sorrow or pain. He was unaware of the reasons of why it was so. When there was none at home, he would play the manual gramophone and announce the play of song exactly like a radio announcer. That alone was his hobby and that alone his game because he had been forbidden to play with the children of the street – his vision being awfully weak! As such, film songs became his playmates. They became his toys too. He copied his favorite songs on the notebook and sang them on the roof. He sang to himself – since loneliness is dumb and could not appreciate the painful and sad songs sung in his own voice, made him sad.

He was often got examined by the doctors. Blind belief regarding the miracles happening is deep-rooted in the psyche of we Indians. His family members too hoped for some miracle to happen at the hands of some doctor.

Once a doctor suggested, "Let him watch a lot many movies. He will come to understand the world through them only otherwise he he will remain an idiot. He will be able to see a lot about the world only on the cinema screen. Let him see movies if you want him to be mentally ripe."

After that day, the doors of cinema hall were wide and freely open for him. he would go to see the movie every week. Some movies he would see twice. Father would be irritated but what could he do. There was hardly any movie of that time he had not seen and one or the other scene of which had not been printed on his mind. That is where the tale of his being a dreamer starts.

He dreamt of fairies in the beginning. But these fairies took him neither to another land nor was he their prince. If the fairies visited him in his dreams, they would first cure his eye-sight with their magic and then made him strong as Dara Singh. He played with them. His whole family began to respect him. He would visit this dream again and again – this dream was most dear to him. he would desire the fulfillment of this dream some day in his heart of hearts. These fairies of his dreams were not from the pictures of books but they were film heroines. The beautiful film heroines visited him in his dreams as fairies, made him as he wanted to be but it wasn't going to be.

One can easily understand his innocence from this that whenever a sadhu came at the door for begging, he thought that the fairies had sent him with the message of their coming. His mother would rebuke him and pulled him as he tried to get near him saying – what can you say about these scoundrel sadhus, they may kidnap the boy. It hurt him badly. He couldn't tell his mother that that sadhu had brought a message from his fairies. Sometimes when he felt tense, he would think why some sadhu doesn't kidnap him. is he not that good that some sadhu kidnaps him. what will he do if someone kidnaps him? then he would start weaving dreams like a braggart. These dreams were in no way different from the film stories when a villain catches a hero with the help of some goons and confines him in a blind room from where the hero escapes just by a miracle or by some good luck.

Our hero became habitual of remaining lost in a world of dreams as time passed. He loved night the most. The arrival of evening delighted him because the time to be in that world, dearest to him and of which he had been deprived, approached nearer. The bitterness of the whole day spread in his eyes like sweet honey. The day was poisonous and the night was honey-sweet. He would open his heart fully to his fairies. Then he would help his fairies in trouble – after all, he had to reward their favors. They had also blessed him with a clear vision and a sound body. In his dreams, he took revenge from his classmates also who teased him and he cried and they delighted in his cries. They would all apologize to him in dreams. He would also make them cry and enjoyed himself.

Friends, he who dreams has to taste their shattering also. Our hero also had enjoyed that taste in his childhood. After cultivating the habit of dreaming, that "IDIOT" read the stories of the greatness of Rama, Krishna, Buddha written in his books and thought he too would become Rama and Buddha. He started weaving this dream. He began imagining his own greatness. The "IDIOT" told about his dream first to his family members and then to his friends. The family members laughed and his friends began mocking at him. the hero couldn't understand. When his story reached the school teachers, he became an object of laughter for them also. "So you would become Ramchander?" The teachers burst into laughter if he said yes. "There goes Ramchander! Ha..ha..ha! blind he is – and would become Ramchander....ha...ha...ha" he listened to these dialogues and passed by his teachers with his head hanging down. He felt ashamed at what he had said.

One day, it crossed all limits. His friends blamed him for the mischief made by them as usual. The school master began to beat him and shouted at him in abusive language – "Say, you bastard, will you become Ram? You mother-fucker, will you be Ram? You bastard, you are there to become Ram?" He realized for the first time while being thrashed that what he wanted to be, they were full of hatred for him. Are those people really that bad and deserving of hatred? How falsely they have been lauded. With his satchel hanging on his back and sobbing, he set out for his home and decided that he would be anything but Ram or Buddha who were the objects of their mockery. It was for the first time that day that that IDIOT had tasted the bitterness of his dream shattered. Who will make him realize that actually they are not bad but these people who are frustrated for not being someone the world could be proud.

He was least interested in studies. No one even motivated him. he would often hear his mother saying," I shall make an offering of one and a quarter rupee if he passes tenth class." He would think that he had to study up to the tenth class only, he will complete somehow. His mother had made up her mind that after he passed matriculation, she would arrange work for him at the cloth shop of one of her relatives. "He will manage himself and what else can be done for him." he wanted to oppose her mother – but couldn't – he didn't want to hurt his mother with his own views. In spite of his great resentment against his mother, he loved her because she alone was there to take care of him. whenever he accompanied his mother to the market, it troubled him a lot getting into the relative's shop to buy clothes. He imagined himself sitting there. It gave him a strange feeling. He didn't know why he never felt bad thinking of unfolding the cloths there to the customers. This is not a hateful scene in any way, though there are worse than this. But who will convince that IDIOT? He returned home, went on the roof to relieve himself by singing some painful film song.

He would often dream of having been chained heavily by someone. He wants to liberate himself from those chains, he is helpless in breaking them, he is crying,

he is doing his best with his weak slim body without doing any harm to them, he is feeling more tightly bound. Even the fairies didn't lad from the heavens to free him. now even the fairies had stopped visiting him in his dreams.

The pain of our hero can be well-gauged from the incident when one evening, he was eating with the family, the same poisonous sentence escaped his mother that he would work at the cloth shop. It escaped his moth also suddenly-"No, I won't sit there. I shall be a doctor."

"haha..haha..will become a doctor!" His elder brother who himself had failed as a science student and was forced to bean arts student in B.A. said in a mocking tone, "Have you ever seen yourself in the mirror? Will be a doctor! I couldn't be a doctor, how can you be a doctor? Hmmm, would become a doctor!"

His elder brother kept jeering at him, his sisters kept enjoying the laugh, mother kept roasting the chapattis and he went on taking his meals with head hanging down as if he were swallowing wet sand. He could never convince his brother that all are not made of the same stuff, that what his brother couldn't do, it was not necessary that he too wouldn't do that...and also that he was different from all.

That night, our hero had to confront dreadful monsters, snakes and crocodiles in a dream. The poor fellow remained engaged in a fight against these horrible creatures, running away from them. Fairies didn't come even then. When he was about to be swallowed by a crocodile in the morning, he woke up with a start. He was perspiring. He had become very dejected that day. He kept singing the whole day – "Call me back, O God, I don't feel at ease in your world." But he found no relief. Whom to talk to? There was none with whom he could open his heart. He has no friend. There is none to comfort him, to encourage him. Nobody had two loving words for him. One day while moving restlessly from one room to another, he happened to find one of the books of his brother. It was a detective novel. He sat reading that unwillingly as he could understand. That novel engrossed him. Oblivious of his own pain, he set out with the hero of that novel in search of that murderer who had murdered an innocent girl. He found a good remedy to escape the pains of daily life.

That is how our hero found another world to rid himself of the daily sufferings – the world of the detective novels. He started reading rented novels – even three novels a day. He had nothing to do with the family, now it was all the better. Whenever, something hurt him, he sang some film song or hid his face in the novels.

He continued to live in a world of his dreams. But now the beautifully charming and tall film heroines replace the fairies and he himself assumed the role of their princes. His dreams turned colorful. He would sing film songs with his heroines and woke up fresh in the morning. The intoxication of these dreams was so maddening that the reality of life disappeared at once from his sight. The film actresses filled the blank of his inner self with everything in such a way that it set out for a quest for him. He was not able to understand what all this was going on which looked for an expression.

Now you may take it as a good luck, not a chance finding of a story-teller like me that our hero with the inspiration of his elder brother he himself had received from one of his college professors that he started reading the literary creations published as pocket books. Starting with Acharya Chatursen, he reached Bedi through Manto. This helped him in understanding himself after reading these litterateurs. It created a feeling of self-confidence in him that he too can do something to be someone. He had some grip over his own situation. He came to realize now why the idea of working at a cloth shop seemed strange to him. he began to realize that he was not born to sit at a shop. He made up his mind to study to become someone! What if his vision is so weak!

The impact of some studies, fresh zeal and zest of youth, somewhat his romantic dreams – all joined to create such a pressure on him that he began to write something – in the current of Neeraj, Sahir Ludhianavi and Bachchan. Urdu poetry seemed closer to his heart – poetry not only expressed his own pains and sufferings but also expressed his romantic relations with the princesses of his dreams. In this way, our IDIOT HERO happened to create another world for himself – the world which is known as the world of poetry, the world of literature. Literature solaced him and also blessed him with the feeling of wisdom and pain that he was all by himself – he had to face and live with all the future obstructions caused by his weal sight all alone. He shared his pains and sorrows with the fairies of his dreams, talked about his dreams, recited his unrhymed couplets to them and wove the dream of being a great Urdu poet. Now who could make this IDIOT gentleman understand that life is not lived in dreaming of film heroines. It is possible to live with dreams but not by losing oneself in dreams. Film heroines can be momentary companions but not for life. But his IDIOT was not ready to understand this truth because this was his only shelter. How could he live if he abandoned that? Shelter is necessary for everyone, isn't it?

The opposition of the family, taunts of society and the mocking jeers of the friends, the main focus of which was his weak vision, he faced them all by running away from them taking shelter in the books, films, film-songs, poetry, beautiful romantic dreams and these alone were his world of comfort and motivation. He had learnt truly that the society took delight in laughing at the handicapped or physically challenged. People in society do look at the handicaps of others but their own dwarfishness remains unseen to them. He also leant that the society was flooded with the idiots, dunces and the callous. A person of sensitivity and understanding is neither valued nor needed. Even after knowing this all, he couldn't rid himself of his own inferiority in reality. Satires of society always stared and were directed at him. he wanted to be an achiever in life so that he could earn a respectable space in the shallow society and his insensitive family. He felt that he had the art of writing which is rarely gifted to some and he would make the best use of it. But our hero had such rooted inferiority that he was not prepared to show his writings to anyone. He didn't want his writing also to be mocked. He loved his creation like a mother who was not ready to listen anything nonsensical about her good-for-nothing son even. He might have heard some words of praise or accepted some suggestions for the improvement of his creation but that poor helpless was confronted with different kinds of hostilities. When he wrote a story for the first time in life and showed it to his family members as the idiot he was, his elder brother read it and had a hearty laugh and proved that the hero had borrowed the plot of the film *Phool aur Patthar* and *Vachan*. The hero was so badly disheartened and dispirited because of his incurable inferiority that he felt that he couldn't write a story. He didn't write a story then for years. He started writing *ghazals* unmindful of his family members as they had not even a remote idea of poetry.

He had a narrow escape even while writing *ghazals.* He happened to show his ghazals in his stupidity to one of his Gold

Medalist professor of Urdu in his town. While smoking a puff of cigarette, he dubbed those couplets as the weakest after listening to which in the college poetry recitation program (*Mushayara*), he had lavishly praised and appreciated him. it was this lavish appreciation that prompted him to show his *ghazal*s to him. Here are three examples of his sharp criticism – the hero wrote," when death comes in hundred ways", he asked why only hundred, why not hundred thousand? Why not even a hundred hundred thousand? Did he come after counting the ways of death? When the hero talked about the poetic idiom, he was provoked-"What do you know? You make me understand the meaning of the poetic idiom?" when the hero said," the earthen lamp (*chiraag* as metaphor) of my eyes", he objected by saying if eyes were a lamp, if eyes were an earthen lamp.. the hero wrote-"Yearning is mine to share my sorrows with someone, let someone come, I sit here." Then his objection was why anyone should come, why he himself doesn't go to some. Then he said, "Poetry(shayari) is not meant for you." Afflicted by inferiority, our hero happened to offer many of his creations to flames. This stupidly innocent idiot couldn't understand that by these measurements, even Mir and Ghalib would be crushed into nothing, so what status he has. It can be hardly imagined how many talents have been crushed before blossoming because of such professors. Our hero escaped because of his own hard studies and earned maturity. Otherwise you are well acquainted with his situation now. In the meanwhile, his sensitivity suffered a fresh wound everyday and he would hide himself somewhere in the corner of his world of dreams. What else could he do?

***

He didn't have to struggle much to seek admission in the college. The family had no economic strains and they thought it would not matter at all if he passes one or two classes more. They were not in a hurry to engage him at the cloth shop. College life had its own charm. He made some friends. His feeling of inner inferiority began to provoke him to take part in the cultural programs in the college. As a result, he began to participate enthusiastically in all such functions. His hidden talent began to express itself. He would participate in the poetry recitation contests, win prizes, sing songs and entertained them all. He began to play roles in dramas – it is a different matter that he was given the role of the accountant only because of his high-numbered glasses. But he was happy – he had been thunderously clapped which bandaged and healed all his wounds. He felt above the rest of the world when he received the prize. He could win the love and respect of all his college-mates because of his zealous participation in the cultural programs in the college. Otherwise the college mates would not have spared this handicapped. It doesn't mean that they didn't feel like teasing him for their sadistic pleasure but none would dare say a word to tease this beloved of the college. It was for the first time in life that he had tasted self-confidence. He would compose poems and couplets. The appreciation of the friends delighted him. his dreams became all the more romantic and went sky-high. He would share his excitement of winning prizes with the princesses of his dreams and felt inspired and motivated to move forward. He was so absorbed in his world that he couldn't even bear the thought of isolating himself from there. If he is not reading a book, he is writing; if not writing, he is singing; if not singing, he is with some princess of his dreams. His condition was still that of his childhood – ignored by the family, and lost in himself, with all his tortures. The only difference now was that then his equipment for play was limited but now it was much more. In spite of all this, he felt deeply sad inside. He felt emptiness somewhere. He wished to have someone who could fill this emptiness with his sweet words. But who would understand the inner being of this IDIOT? Whom to convince? He was extremely lonely and sad on a journey in the desert of life with all the external dazzle.

He initiated such a step in his effort to face society to rid himself of his inner emptiness which is discussed even today in society as a proof of his idiocy. He had been deeply influenced by some of his college professors for their scientific outlook. They awakened him to the widespread corruption in society, inhuman conduct of the leaders etc. which were confirmed by their being reported in the newspapers. That IDIOT also felt like doing something to end corruption in society. He entertained a strong desire like the film heroes after watching movies. It was beyond him as to what to do. He studied the life-stories of revolutionaries like Chander Shekhar Azad and Bhagat Singh in those very days. These biographies inspired him to create an organization the terror of which may either kill or reform all the corrupt leaders and officials of the country. He began to strongly feel that people like Azad and Bhagat Singh are needed again today. They alone could make this India stuck badly in this rotten swamp a Heaven again. He was a born dreamer and began dreaming that he had made his country again a Paradise. The leaders of the country have become clean, simple and non-violent completely – live their life on their honest income. His this dream also became dear to him with the dreams of singing love songs with his beloved film heroines as this also raised him to heroism in society.

He needed the help of some people to make this his dream a reality. So he thought of speaking about this first to his friend with whom he had a common thinking and discussed the dismal social conditions for hours and who himself was unhappy with such disgusting social conditions. He shared with his friend in a convincing manner his idea of his imagined organization. His friend also listened to him carefully and seriously. After listening to the hero, he reflected for some time and then with his hand on his shoulder, said, " Yaar, you are absolutely right. You are absolutely genuine in what you say. Such an organization is surely needed which pledges itself to serve the country above its personal selfish interests. But, my dear friend, this is not practicable in spite of its being a true, pure and sacred feeling. Look, I'm saying it as your well-wisher that this idea of organization you have shared with me but, for God's sake, don't share it with anybody else. If you don't check yourself, this government machinery will throw you in the jail as a Naxalite. It won't matter much if they kill you. Every revolutionary is a Naxalite today. The greatest danger to the government today is only from Azad and Bhagat Singh. So they will suppress you first like the British. Had these great patriots been alive today, they would have committed suicide thinking that they fought against the British for this country or the government would have thrown them into jail to rot. When such conditions persist, what would you do? You forget this dream. None will stand with you. If someone stands, he will have his own selfish interest. Take care of yourself. I respect your feelings. Otherwise also, you are not made of that stuff that you may do this all."

His friend convinced him that politics has been criminalized today. It is necessary to seek the help of some party to do something. Nothing is possible without this. Seeking help of some party means to agree with their terms and conditions and thus all your thinking, your ideals and determination will be mortgaged to them.

Our hero was fear-stricken on hearing all this. He felt that these politicians would get him killed cashing in on his ideology.

His friend's explanation and advice disappointed him completely. He realized that his dream cannot be fulfilled. But he doesn't know why his friend seemed wrong though he was realistic. He thought of trying again. He spoke to many friends. All assured him of their help on his face but they laughed loudly as he turned his face. They would jeer at him in his absence – "What a great patriot! Wants to become Bhagat Singh! A lifeless soul is out to be a revolutionary." All began to tease and irritate him, as it spread, saying, "Hello, dear patriot?', "How are you, dear revolutionary?" "How are you, dear disciple of Bhagat

Singh?" his heart was shattered. He was isolated all the more. He felt that the whole world was stoning him with taunts. It soon spread to the whole city.

He had not yet come to himself that his father told him one evening that he was close to the policemen, they have told him as a friend that the detective police was after him. his trying to take part in ant-social activities and its information is with the government. The police wants him to desist from such activities.

That evening, his father scolded him so furiously that he was shaken. What had he not to listen that day? He is insane born to bring a bad name to the family. He should have died at birth. He will be happy to see his parents in the jail. Kill your whole family first if you love to be a revolutionary that much! He can't kill a fly even and is out to be a revolutionary. He cannot bear even a slap of the police and you dream of being a Bhagat Singh. He won't be able to spend even two days in the jail. He will forget all patriotism in jail. He received many gifts of the metaphorical filthy abuses that evening-"Stupid, donkey, idiot, insane, loafer…!" mother kept weeping saying that he is born to be a trouble for us.

Our hero kept weeping the whole of that night. He had never endured so much torture. This pain was unbearable for him. he couldn't understand what evil he had done that the whole society and the whole family have turned against him. he has dreamt only of keeping his country clean. He wanted to die. He can't do anything in such a situation. He couldn't understand that the whole society was against evil but whoever tried to reform and clean it, was crushed. What a world this is that thrashes him who wants to be Ram and jails him who wants to be Bhagat Singh. He was intensely pained at the world's difference between what the world says and what it does. That night, many scorpian questions kept stinging him and he kept bearing the pain. The pain of wound of his shattered dream was so deep that he couldn't come to his senses. None will convince this IDIOT that we are all used to living in this polluted environment that we won't be able to live for long in clean, pollution-free environment. Nobody wants a change. This is convenient for all. This country has become paralytic now and nothing can be done. It can die its death only.

The necessary outcome of this shattered dream of our hero was that feeling intensely pained and tense at the failure of his being many-sided, he was confined to himself with his loneliness, sorrow and emptiness. He took a painful decision that he would never think of reforming a little this society, not to talk of changing it. This decision troubled him all his life. But he was helpless. Of course, he resolved certainly and foolishly to be honest and truthful for himself. So he remained full of sadness, loneliness and emptiness as before.

Friends, I know that you would be smiling or laughing at the idiocy of this hero and looking for an opportunity to say that it doesn't matter if this story-teller couldn't make this hero a revolutionary, he has become at least a lover-hero. I know this also that if you are showing utmost patience in reading this tale, it is with hope of the introduction of a heroine who would add romance to the tale. A story without a heroine is boring and tiring. Otherwise also, a story without a heroine is colorless. I'm quite aware of all these reasons and know that if the hero were not introduced to the heroine at this age, you would stop reading this tale. Friends, rest assured that I don't have even a remote idea of introducing this IDIOT to a heroine. You alone tell me if anybody can fall in love with an IDIOT. Our hero was suffering from extreme inferiority complex in view of his normal complexion and his high-numbered glasses. He was convinced that no girl could fall in love with him. this fact had assumed its own sanctity. So he had accepted the fact that he had to live all his life with the film heroines. His long association with the charming fairies and then with the film-heroines since his childhood, he had quite a high touchstone of beauty. Now the thought of love in this IDIOT's life in such a situation was a curse. Better you excuse me for my inability to introduce you to a heroine. You are angry with me? Okay! Don't be annoyed with me. Readers like you are difficult to find. I shall write for whom if I annoy you. How shall I feed my family? Who will encourage my ego? There are only one or two truthful who are uncaring for the readers. Others tell lies. All writers look for a large number of readers. Your help alone feeds my family. So I shall have to respect your love of the romance or your romantic leaning. If I have to change the basic plot of the tale to feed your interests, I shall not hesitate – it is somewhat immaterial to introduce love and romance in it. I feel fortunate that my readers expected only love-story from me whereas their romantic taste has no end – it could have demanded some vulgar touch. Well, you want some romantic strain for the satisfaction of your inherent taste. That's fine. Obeying you is my first and foremost duty since you are like a god for a poor story-teller like me. So here I present the heroine respecting the strong desire of my readers. Dear readers, the appearance of a heroine is going to give a different turn to the tale – even to the life of the hero – and I would not be blamed for this. It is in your romantic interest which has the temptation to see even the IDIOT in love.

The friend of the hero's sister will have to be necessarily shown to the heroine to make their meeting possible. Friends dear, try to understand this compelling necessity – the hero has a weak sight – what will he gain if he is a philanderer? Above all this is his inferiority complex. This is only suitable that the hero's sister was her friend. She was the most beautiful of all her friends. There was melody and echo like that of Asha Bhonsale in her voice. That heroine catered to the hero's love of beauty to some extent and you may give her any name – Seema, Veena, Aabha, Radha, Shobha, Sarla, Vimla, hema or Neela-or any other. Whenever she came, he would be a hero to enchant his inner being with the sweet melody of the heroine's voice in his ears. He would enjoy her beauty too if there was an opportunity.

The heroine's love of singing alone brought the hero closer to her. The heroine knew that the hero composed couplets. The heroine felt the need of a good ghazal to be recited at the preparations for the Youth Festival in the college. She requested the hero not only for a ghazal but also for some couplet unheard by anybody obviously, she wanted to recite as her own.

Now you yourself imagine the position of the hero. That was the finest day of his life and he had felt for the first time that he was alive. The sea of suppressed emotions began to swell in him. it was for the first time that some charming beauty had asked for something from him in her magical voice. He would have sacrificed his life then. Such was the condition of that poor fellow! Although, it was simply-"She looked with a smile, I took it as her love." But the hero was unaware of all this. He worked hard on the selection of a beautiful ghazal of some famous Urdu poet to be given to her with his own ten-fifteen couplets well-written in beautiful hand.

The readers would certainly like to know why the hero didn't give his own ghazal. You have no right to ask this question because you had desired to introduce the context of love. There would come such jerks on the way. No, no, you needn't be apologetic – you are my readers. Your question is genuine. The truth is that the hero had no knowledge of the technique of writing a ghazal – he didn't know how to attempt at the same time – he learnt all this at a later stage. Then he regarded his unrhymed couplets also as perfect. Now about the heroine – even she had no idea of all this. She was fond of writing couplets in her diary in the excitement of youth. Whether it was the gentleness, innocence or stupidity of the hero – whatever you may think – he didn't give the borrowed or stolen couplets as his own to fascinate the heroine. He was so scared of being exposed that he couldn't do this even if he wanted. Who would have told this IDIOT that deceptive lies are loved more in daily life than pure gold. Love-affairs begin, bloom and end mostly on this basis. There are a few idiots who languish in life accepting lies as truth, the rest live a life of pleasures.

In the meanwhile, let me use another small film technique to bring the context of romance back on the track. The heroine won the first prize in the Youth Festival by reciting the *ghaza*l. It's credit goes also to the tune set in the *raag* tradition also along with the heroine. The couplets of the *ghazal* come at the third place though the audience showered lavish praises on the voice of the heroine and the couplets. Now the heroine had greater respect for the hero and the hero was so overwhelmed as if he had won the prize. The heroine fully appreciated his *ghaza*l and the couplets which sent the hero on cloud nine.

It was for the first time that the heroine replaced the film heroines in hero's dreams. She cast a spell on the life of the hero. After all, it was the first love. He began to be uneasy. He would look to her coming to him. now the heroine began to borrow novels from him to read. The hero had only those few moments when she stood beside him while selecting novels from the almirah. She appreciated his poems and couplets and motivated him to write more and more. This alone was the reason that she settled firmly in his veins. The heroine alone had appreciated his talent and that too in her sweet lilting voice. The hero longed, not for his praise but for the appreciation of his talent; the heroine fulfilled that yearning. The hero felt that it was she alone who has recognized him. it was as if the hero had found the purpose of living. The heroine showed not only respect in the recognition of his talent but also inspired him to improve upon it further. The more he thought of the heroine, the more he felt involved with her. If at all the heroine said, " I have very deep respect for you", he would trace countless meanings in that. He was an IDIOT at last! Had it been in his power, he would have engraved this dialogue of the heroine on every wall of the city, on every road-"Once you feel respect for someone, it is never lost. I can forget everyone but not you!" These honey-dipped dialogues had gone down his very soul!

Now the hero began to yearn to speak those very frequently repeated dialogues to the very soul of his life. He lost his appetite. He often felt restless. He had sleepless nights. He was worried to think if she refused, how would he live? And then what would happen? He didn't want to lose her. He had got the only one companion to for happiness in life. He was satisfied with one-sided love only. There is no fear of any accidental fall!

Like other middle class heroes, our hero too might have spent his life in one-sided love. But he was overwhelmed with emotions in the first place. He used to feel that if he didn't express himself, he will certainly go mad. Secondly, since this context has been created to please my readers, this has to be developed further. It was for the first time that the desire to live had risen in the IDIOT. Life had seemed meaningful to him for the first time. He had realized for the first time that he had a talent which everyone doesn't have, what if his eyesight was weak. He had liked himself for the first time otherwise he had died in his degraded self. Only he knows how many dreams he had woven for his heroine. He took his birth as a blessing. He was full of zeal and passionate energy, although the heroine had not given any such hint. Of course, she used to come to his home as a family member. She rightfully opened his almirah of books and kept looking at them. The hero had not given this right even to his family whereas the heroine had enjoyed this right on her own. The hero immensely liked her opening his almirah and reading his poems in the note-book. This action of the heroine was the hero's greatest bliss.

After remaining highly tense for some days when it became unbearable, the hero decided to speak those two-three usual sentences that had lost their meaning to the heroine. He bought a notebook from the market. Therein he wrote some of his own and some borrowed interesting couplets in beautiful hand. Then he wrote the heroine's name on the top of a paper, then his own two couplets and registered his name at the bottom. The readers must be curious to know about those couplets. They can't be described here, their collection can be published separately. Yes, the two couplets she wrote to express her love, I mention here-knowing it well that all are not interested in poetry. I have corrected the rhythmic tone of these couplets so that you are impressed by the hero. Here are the couplets-

"The desire to live woke up only after seeing you,
I learnt the meaning of life after seeing you?
Embrace, if you wish; reject, if you wish,
I have appeared before you as a life!"

Here it can be very apt to know why this IDIOT hero who had been spending his life by singing film songs, singing them with the film actresses in his dreams, didn't express his love for the heroine by singing a film song. Why he didn't woo his love by singing the most popular songs like-

"What should I say to you, O my love, you can see my condition." Or

"I shall be obliged if you allow me to say what I want to." Or

"How I should say that I love you." Or

Then Sahir's most sung – "I have no control over my love, even then you tell me I should love you or not." In fact the hero was going to do this but he felt that he should express himself in his talent she respects the most. Only they shelter themselves in songs who know nothing else. He will express himself in his words only.

As the heroine came, he said while offering that notebook with his beating heart and trembling hands," I have specially prepared it for you. You keep it for yourself. This is my present to you. There is one page also, do read it. That is actually the expression of my feelings for you. Will you respond?" he was gone in the excitement of uttering this single sentence. He ran away from that almirah where the heroine stood with a notebook with her head hanging down. Those readers who have passed through such a situation can understand such restlessness. I leave it to the imagination of the readers whether the heroine read that paper there or at her home.

The heroine didn't come for the next three days. You just judge the condition of this hero. He again lost his appetite. His own world was seen biting him. Countless desires were there to entangle him. at last, he decided that he won't choose to live if the heroine rejected him. there was nothing else in his life. He spent the night weeping to himself. How he should know why the heroine had not come and began to repent at showing his love to her. Why should she accept him? what would he be able to give her? He is burden on himself. He was face to face with the tragedy of the hero. His loneliness since his childhood, the taunts of the people, his unwanted talent, the feeling of disrespect and mockery for the talent – who know how he endured again in those three days since it happened.

When she came on the third day, she returned his novels to him. The heroine happened to see a paper stuck in one of the novels. He was puzzled. The heroine also didn't stay that day – she left. The hero took out that page with his beating heart and trembling hands after she was gone. The heroine had written in her beautiful hand-"You give all your sorrows and tensions to me" and "Give all your sorrows to me if you love me" on the basis of the openings of film songs for the first and the last time a couplet. I write here that couplet in corrected form-

"All your sorrows you give to me,
This is the only bliss I wish from you."

You cannot realize the hero's ecstasy. The whole world's joys couldn't express that ecstasy. She was the first maiden beauty of his life which gave him fresh current of life. Gratitude can be shown to the heroine for bringing this immense delight in hero's life. What can be a greater bliss than this if he can spend a few moments of delight for the hero after his life of loneliness and torture since his childhood. He felt like sharing his ecstasy. Someone loves him too – he wanted to tell this to the whole world. He wanted to share his delight with his friends. But he could not do so even though he was willing because it was only a few days ago that he spoke about his love to one of his dearest friends and he jeered at him-"This is a lie. Not even a she-donkey can love that ugly fellow." The hero had been shaken. Later on his friend had been heartily laughed at in the friendly gang on this issue. The hero became conscious – who will believe him? he felt broken at heart. Although he had learnt by rote the couplet of the heroine, yet he would read again and again the words written on that paper. Who knows how comforting were those two couplets in the hero's own hand to her? For the first time, he had known such restlessness, such peace and such embracive love. He wanted to have the whole sky in his arms.

Some of my intellectual readers may find it hard to digest to think how a beautiful maiden can fall in love with our IDIOT hero with too ordinary appearance with high-numbered glasses! This is a film-trick. A wealthy beauty may fall in love with a village rustic in the films – or a wealthy loafer can wink at a village milk maid. It happens nowhere in actual life. You seem to be correct, dear friends. If you trouble yourself to look around to find that the whole world is flooded with mismatches. Here a handsome husband has an ugly-looking wife; and there it is irritating to think why a beautiful wife chose to marry a disgusting husband? And if you come across beautiful match at the physical level, you will a terrible mental gap in them. To be brief, you will find everywhere such mismatches only.

If you find this reason unconvincing, just have a look into the psyche of the heroine. She didn't give her consent at once and spent three days reflecting on this. Secondly, the heroine was well aware of the philanderers hovering around her with their sexy looks. Since she was not precocious by nature, she felt calm and serious. She found the hero different from others. She was fully convinced that the hero was a simple-minded and brilliantly talented young man who never has any feeling of sexual desire at the sight of a beautiful girl before him. He has the sense of being respectful to a beauty standing before him. Her fascination lay in the hero's talent. Thirdly, for some girls, the virtues of the boy are more important than his handsomeness. The heroine was mature in this respect and no girl would ever reject him who seeks her love so sensibly. Our heroine was not arrogant of her beauty and virtues. Had she been so, she would have rejected not only this hero but many heroes. I know that these reasons are enough to justify this mismatched love-affair. If it doesn't satisfy you even now, do think of it as a film trick.

The heroine noticed some pleasant changes in the hero. He not only stays happy now but also has become conscious of his dress-up. He has greater self-confidence in him now than before. Now he writes better. The best she liked in the hero was his transparency. He was the same in and out. He was extremely innocent, emotional and imaginative. The inner beauty of the hero had impressed the heroine. Then the hero gave to her his most secretive writing – his diary – wherein he had a living presence with all his pains, inferiorities, tensions, sorrows and desires. The heroine went on reading feeling astonished how come that this boy is still alive. Our emotional heroine felt more attached with him after reading the diary. She felt that it would not be enough if she showers all her true love on him. She was convinced about the hero's capability to move forward amazingly. He needs only inspiration. She said something to the hero on reading her diary and her own emotionality that stayed unfulfilled with him all his life-"Only love and trust are the most important in life. I shall give only that to you."

The hero too was at his best. That IDIOT also told her that she alone is the first and the last girl of his life. He cannot think of anybody else even in his dreams and won't be able to do so. He not only loves her but also idolizes her. She would always be there in his creations. She is there whenever he writes. She is the only bliss of his life. He can do even the impossible for her. She is his inspiration. She is his poetry. He won't do anything in life which may disgrace her. All these dialogues of the hero may have been inspired by Mohan Rakesh's play "*Aashad ka ek Din*" and Ageya's "*Shekhar Ek Jivani*" read in those days but these readers casting a plain look at this life know it well that these are not mere emotions. These dialogues are his plain truth. His emotionality hides all his life. I may make it clear here that even after being loved by the heroine, the hero never had any physical contact with her, never tried to kiss her like the lovers of today whereas today love begins with this. It doesn't mean that the hero didn't want to do that, he didn't want to embrace her, he didn't want to kiss her, but a boy from a noble family is brought up and is a slave to higher values, *sanskaar.* Secondly, that IDIOT was under the deep influence of the old film heroes who sang romantic songs from a distance of two yards! To be brief, their love was confined to conversation.

Now the heroine began to make him aware that he had to become a great man and he was not born to sit at a cloth shop. He can do all which a normal capable man does. He has to study hard, he has to write a lot – he has to earn a name. he has to create a space for himself in the world. He is far better than most of the people in the world, far higher. He has to prove his identity. He is wise, he is capable – what else is needed to be great. She will always stand with the hero. He has to do this all even if she is not there otherwise she would think that the friendship was all a waste. She won't be able to bear this all. All her hopes now rest on the hero. Friends, I feel like taking pride in the luck of the hero. It would have been something truly great if this story-teller had such an inspiration!

Well, the heroine's inspiration sent a fresh current of energy making the hero youthful. He started dreaming of becoming a great man – he dreamt that he had left behind all his obstacles and the heroine watches him with a charming smile. He would dream of flying in the heavens with his heroine and the stunned people are watching them from below. The heroine put life into the stagnant energy of the hero. Everybody is blessed with such inspiration in life.

Two tragedies occurred in the hero's life before the hero could take off. One was that the hero lost in dreams failed. There was only one dialogue uttered for long in the family – "We knew it already that he would fail. The whole day busy with novels, films, songs – he had no time for studies. We knew that he won't study. His sitting on the cloth shop would have been better." This failure made the hero tense. He had no justification to give. His sadness, dejection, pain, loneliness were again with him. the heroine's encouragement alone was his little comfort. The heroine felt that the hero himself was somewhere responsible for his situation. There was truth in it. He was lost more talking with the heroine in imagination that he studied. The hero held himself responsible completely. He had his inspiration with him, so he drank the poison of this wound. He resolved that now he won't let such defeat occur again. It was his promise with his inspiration. The shooting taunts of the family and society couldn't hurt him more this time due to the heroine's inspiration.

But the heroine was in deep sorrow somewhere. She wept bitterly when she was alone. What else should she do? She wished from her very heart that this simple-minded lovely young man cursed by the humiliations and inferiorities who has come in her life and whom she loves with all her heart and at whose genius she offers flowers, should stay for some more years in her life. The hero should be on the track; thereafter anything may happen to her. But she remained helpless with all her efforts. She felt that she was pushing the hero into the jaws of death. She knew that the hero was totally dependent on her and he won't be able to bear this setback. She cannot die – this setback would destroy all, the possibilities of saving the hero. She cannot elope with the hero – the hero is not in a position to take this risk. Then what should she do? She would start weeping when there was no way out. She tried her best to persuade her father to let her pass B. A. at least. But all her entreaties fell flat on her dictatorial father. Her marriage had been fixed with a New York-settled boy who happened to be her elder brother's friend. He had visited India only for three weeks. The heroinc knew all this would happen one day because when will the hero be in a position to seek anybody's hand in marriage – now nothing can be thought about it for four or five years. It was not at all possible that her autocratic father would delay her marriage. She was aware of the consequences of this love-affair but this end will come so soon before her, she had never imagined. She was not worried about herself. She was worried about the hero who had not known any happiness of life so far. What will become of him? Who will look after him – such thoughts troubled her and she began to weep.

The hero judged the sadness of the heroine. If judged, he was full of doubts. The heroine had to come out with the truth. The hero didn't turn into stone-like but actually became a stone. She had been telling that stone that life was not confined to her only. The hero must honor his commitment. He has to stand by and stand for himself and move forward. What if she was not near – she would always look to him. He will have to endure this shock. She herself is enduring this shock for him. I wish he were so strong that she could go with him! The hero has to decide the course of his life on his own. Her own days are numbered. She is the only remaining hope of her life. He has to be true to this hope by keeping his word. It is not only her hope but she is sure also that he won't disappoint her.

The first thing the hero did was that he tore into pieces all his notebooks in which he had written his poems. He had written some stories also – he destroyed them too. These are all meaningless in the absence of a person who made them possible with her loving inspiration! When even this didn't end his resentment, he collected all those pieces in the envelop and sent them to the heroine.

The heroine was stunned to see them. She didn't know what to do for some moments. She kept looking at those pieces with curious eyes. Then she burst into tears. What should she do? How can she help that stupid boy? How could she stop him from ruining himself. How she could take him out of this tragic happening? She knew it well that it couldn't be left to time to heal this wound in case of the hero.

When she came to meet the hero, he not only refused to talk to her but also left home. The heroine was extremely sad. She felt that the hero will certainly ruin himself. This thought alone was most painful for the heroine and this was the most dangerous too. Sad and dejected heroine returned home. She wanted to cry but couldn't. She would wake up with a start at night. She had a feeling of uneasiness on waking up. She knew that the hero was on the verge where anything was possible. She would spend her night in restlessness with all these doubts. She again tried twice to talk to the hero. But the hero shirked facing her. She was aware of the hero's condition, so she had no grudge against him. if at all she had a grudge, it was with herself and her circumstances. When there was no way in sight, she addressed a letter to the hero – the ever-first letter of her life! It would be unjust to the structure of the story to mention that long letter completely here – so I mention in brief the essence of that letter here. Otherwise I hope that readers won't accept-

"I know that you are very angry with me. I should write or speak something to you – you have denied all these rights to me today. I had never expected this day to arrive in my life. I understand that I am responsible for all your sorrow and pain. You will never forgive me. – sorrow and pain will stay with you always, I know. But why are you ruining yourself? Why are you torturing yourself by destroying your creations? This is my lasting hope that you loved me, shall love me and always love me. But when you have come to realize that I'm undeserving of all this, what is the use of doing this?"

After writing all about here and there, the heroine wrote something meaningful in detail which is attuned to film-style precisely-" This is just in no way for man to desert the whole world for someone." The heroine repeated her frequent previous self – he has to move ahead! He had promised to the heroine to be some envious achiever. He has to keep his promise. He has not to look to anyone for shelter. He is so capable that he an stand for himself. Life never stops with the departure of someone. She will always look to him with a focused mind. She will languish all her life, if he idles himself away.

"What else should I write, keep moving on the journey of your life with a vibrant heart. Don't be disheartened by the obstacles. My good wishes will always be with you. My soul will shower blessings on you even after I die. Be a great write one day. Then remember my good wishes. I shall be the happiest of the soul even after death that day…in the end, my only humble request to you is that you should not destroy your poems and diary if you really love me. At least, keep them safe for those who love you. My love is always there for you. Understand my helplessness. Punish me not by not talking to me. I need a promise from you that you won't do any such thing that may make it hard even to breathe when I go away from you. If you want this, lo, you do whatever you like, you are free. I have nothing more to write. Give me my right once to talk to you."

The hero burst into tears. All his anger was washed away in tears. Reading a letter would bring tears in his eyes. Again he read the letter and wept bitterly. A psychiatrist would agree with me that the hero would have been in the lunatic asylum if the heroine had not written a letter to him and he had not wept bitterly.

Then they both met. For the last time! The heroine used her persuasion powerfully and also wept continuously and the hero had seen his inspiration crying for the first time. He cried in pain. What else he could do except committing himself in that emotional stateand the IDIOT promised to keep living, go on writing, not to tear away his writings and move forward. That is different that he would interrupt himself by saying how he would live without her. The heroine kept telling him not to waste his life for her sake. She is leaving him in the midst. It will sadden her all her life. She herself doesn't want to live anymore as whatever little dreams she had, were shattered. But she will remain alive for the hero. Now they have to live for each other. She has high hopes from the hero. She was leaving with them all buried in her bosom.

And then that bird flew away. The hero remained even now where he was. It seemed to him that he had a romantic dream and now there he found pitch dark as he woke up. How shall he walk even two steps in such darkness? His life had lost its meaning and purpose.

Now the hero started smoking and loafing about the whole day. He became habitual of cursing society over trifles. He became very obstinate and irritating. Cigarette-smoking increased. He wanted to be afflicted with some disease so that he leaves this world. He started drinking also but couldn't be an addict because he didn't want to hurt his mother who alone was in pain after the heroine. Incapable of understanding the complex mentality of her IDIOT son, she also began saying that her son never let her live a day of happiness. God knows what would become of him? the hero listened and a satirical smile spread on his face. He didn't care for anybody. The IDIOT thought of breaking his promise given to the heroine once or twice by being a wise man. Also went to the railway track – but couldn't commit suicide. The same despair and commitment returned to him. He again took to smoking, drinking and heaps of abuses on society. He had abandoned writing. If at all he wrote, it was to vent his anger in his diary. Who else was there with whom he could share his sorrow.

Then he happened to see the heroine weeping in a dream. In her cries, she kept complaining that the hero had not kept his word. She is unhappy and is alive on the hope that the hero would keep his promise. If the hero has to do all this, she had no purpose of being alive. She kept weeping and sobbing. There was none to wipe her tears. The hero woke up with a start. That was merely a dream but he felt even today as if the heroine had really come. It happens sometimes that there is no gap between dream and reality. Both coincide with each other. The hero began to loiter outside uneasily in the verandah. He kept smoking continuously. He had surrendered himself completely to the heroine. It came to him that the society wants him to do what he is doing. This is the natural reaction of society. Unsuccessful lovers do only this. Should he betray the heroine? She used to say that he had to fight against society without expecting anybody to help him. he is pursuing the path accepted by society. The heroine's face wet with tears appeared before him. He heaved a cold sigh and looked at the sky – dawn was coming, morning was not far. The hero took it as the new morning of his life.

Friends, I feel compelled to pause here. The reason being that the readers of romantic leanings are many at whose request, I introduced this love-story unwillingly. Now the same readers complain that it didn't delight them. You know that I have not opened a *halwai* shop to feed them with funnel cakes (*jalebis*) of love. It is not good to play with the emotions of others. Some readers say that this last context should have been a little longer. I have save the hero with great difficulty from the jaws of death and these readers want greater delight in playing with and prolonging the fatal emotions of the hero. What humans we are! The hero is dying and we want enjoyment – how great is our sensitivity! What a clear instance of sadistic pleasure. Is it our tendency working somewhere to see others languishing in love by the basic cause of betrayal in love? Is it not the habit of delighting in all that is seen in society except love and the feeling of belonging? Aristotle gave us the principle of stoicism and we made it as our tendency to delight. How great! Perhaps it is for this reason that some mischievous readers have not maliciously asked if the hero who used to sing sad film songs on the roof in his childhood has not sung branded songs in separation from the heroine – lo, my life companion is gone ending the tale or weeping over the tale of false love, hurt deeply and cursing the youth? Surely he sang! In this context, I shall have no objection if you include all heart-rending songs of deep sorrow and pain played by the renowned announcers, especially by Anwaar Anjum, in the All India Radio's listeners' most requested Urdu program. That helpless fellow had no other way to relieve himself. He couldn't be *Devdas* with his *Devdasia* mindset. You may say jokingly – after all, he is an IDIOT!

Some readers took it is as an ordinary love story. What should I do with this objection? Otherwise, what unusual is there in love? Even in the basis of the extraordinary love, there is ordinariness because love is either fulfilled or failed. From where and how to introduce something new in it? Some people begin to think of it as childishness after some age and some forget it. At the time of writing this tale, I had no claims of this love-story being unusual to make. His tale is not yet complete too. My pain is that those for whose sake I did this all, even they were not happy and instead threw some dialogues at me. I lost myself in an effort to please my readers. Now when I have done a wrong, I feel helpless in carrying it forward. I don't have any other way than to make love as a symbol. So dear readers, the story-teller has accepted the heroine as only a symbol of inspiration in the same way as Kabir called her Maya, Jayashankar Prasad Shraddha as heart and Ira as intellect, Dinkar has treated Pururava and Urvashi as symbols of antique man and woman. How can the IDIOT be fated to have a beloved in reality?

Thereafter, the hero never looked back. After passing B. A., his obstinacy took him to do M. A. he took up again his pen. A new brilliance, fresh feeling and depth spontaneously came in his writing. His inner being would energize itself when he was lost in the dreams of the heroine and talking to her for hours in loneliness, in imagination. He had no other way. What else he had? He had loved the heroine from the very core of his being. She had become such a painful yearning from which he couldn't liberate himself all his life. It was sure to happen with this innocent single-minded IDIOT.

The heroine would write a letter addressed to the hero's sister. There used to be invariably one or two lines in that-"Is the hero studying? Does he write or not? Do send if there is any of his creation." The hero knew that she wrote letters only to find an answer to these lines. He felt as if the heroine had been reminding him continuously of his promise. She wanted to know about his condition. The hero liked this anxiety of the heroine. It was enough for him. but there was a distance rising in the letters of the heroine with time. The hero's sister to whom the letters were addressed was also married. Again the hero was left to himself with none to look to. But he was moving ahead with the self-confidence he had earned. He knew that he won't receive a setback now. It doesn't mean that he didn't feel himself broken and shattered. Even today he had nobody to share his heart with anybody. Even now, he had a companion in his diary or that heroine of his dreams with whom he shared all his tensions.

He had another hurt when he was still in M. A. his mother died suddenly of heart failure. She alone was there in the family whom the hero loved not only as a mother but also genuinely because it was the hero only who understood her pains in the family and assured her, "You don't worry at all, it would be fine. Let me be on job. Then you will stay happily with me." The elder brother and his wife were not on good terms with the mother. The hero lost his only hope in the death of the mother. He was absolutely lonely now. He felt like an orphan though the father, bother and bhabhi were there. He faced the absurdity of life in the naked form. Even after seeing the bitter realities of life with the naked eye, he was now lost in himself, a dreamer listening to film songs. An IDIOT he was after all! Life wanted him to be cunning, a liar, loud-mouthed but he couldn't be like that. An IDIOT at last!

The death of his mother shattered him emotionally. He would be lost in his thoughts in loneliness and remain tense. He had abandoned his studies. Again the same darkness of future horrified him. there was none to comfort and console him. Amidst those tensions, he began to tell himself – he has to honor the promise he made to the heroine. The hero felt that if he didn't lose himself in his studies, he would certainly go mad. These two severe setbacks were enough to disturb his mental balance. He would think in his loneliness who was there for whom he should live. He began to feel shaky again. Even his resolve was also shaking. He sank himself in his studies. This was the only way to get through this situation, he thought. He studied and listened to songs. The melodious voice of Asha Bhonsale gave him the feeling of his heroine being beside him. This was the only escape route to forget the death of his mother and he used it to the full.

He tasted the fruit of losing himself in his studies very soon. His vision which was already very weak began to sound the alarm bells. The hero went to the well-known eye-specialist of the town who was quite familiar with him and his brilliant capability.

"Why do you absorb yourself too much in studies?" the doctor said in extreme pain and heaving a dep cold sigh, he said,

"If your eye-sight had been normal, who knows what you would have achieved? It is the Wil of God!" He prescribed the medicine. The hero would laugh within. What should he say why he studies that hard? What should he say that a lava rises in him. The doctor had referred him to a renowned PGI Eye-specialist, Dr. Jain, in view of his disturbing eye-sight. Dr. Jain was astonished when he came to learn about his studying in M.A. and his being a literatteur. "Had you come to me two months before, you would have been a subject of research with me. I have just guided one of my scholars for research – on people like you. Look, it is not good for you to be ambitious like normal people and compete with them. You should stay happy with whatever you have studied. It is astonishing for me that you have gone that far in studies and are 'mentally intelligent'. Usually it doesn't happen. You vision is so weak that it is not proper for you to be absorbed in reading and writing. You should go in for supervisory check-up. I cannot do anything for you. I'm sorry." The hero returned with only a prescription. He didn't go by the advice of Dr. Jain. He kept reading and writing. He knew it since long that no one could help him. There was some suicidal tendency in him which motivated him to read and write. The absence of his heroine haunted him. Why did she leave him to his care only? He could neither go to her nor he could invite her. It would sometimes irritate him why he committed himself to his heroine to move forward and stay alive. What became of the heroine's promise of love and trust? She has forgotten her promise and why he is keeping his promise. But thinking of the heroine in that way hurt him. Friends, who will tell the IDIOT that promises are meant to break. This world would have been really different if all had been there to be gentlemen in keeping their promises like the IDIOT! This world is as we see it because it is full of promise-breakers, taking false oaths and tongue-twisters. The world prospers with such people!

The path of the hero was not clear even after doing M.A. he had resolved to be a Professor – in spite of his weal vision. No other job seemed to suit his interests. The elder brother had complete control over the father's cinema house. He wanted to create his own course. Cinema fascinated him but not cinema hall. Literature had become his life itself. He thought of doing Ph. D to be a Professor. This created a stir at home when they learnt about his this desire. Obviously, the elder brother and his wife now wanted the hero to stand upto take care of his own. How long will he continue to be fed without doing anything. There were no economic strains as such. Even then the hero's way of life was an eyesore to all.

Father respected his wish for the first and the last time and the elder brother had to consent to his wish for doing Ph. D. he was damn happy that day as the way in which his desire to be a doctor was crushed in childhood, it was going to be fulfilled now, may not be that way. The irrepressible desire in his unconscious was there which woke up at the sight of the opportunity, yet there was the suicidal tendency also which was provoking him to wish that his vision becomes worst and he commits suicide. He had firmly resolved that being all alone in his life would not seek shelter anywhere. Not the least after becoming blind. His ego didn't accept it. Who would make this poor fellow realize that this world is flooded with only the blind and all are busy in this race of the blind. That is why all are on the look out for shelters. All have shelters. All are in the habit of walking with crutches. However, these crutches are not visible. Hence all are blind. That IDIOT alone has no crutch to help himself. The heroine is there but only an inspiration. Only the person with sight will differentiate between the crutch and inspiration.

The whole family lineage had started respecting him while he was in M. A. because he was the first person who had passed M.A. the hero was conscious of this and happy too. All relatives determined to engage him in the cloth shop were now respectful to him. With all this in mind, the hero remained confined within himself as he had not yet achieved his goal. On the other side, he his published creations had made him highly discussed. This also forced all his family members to treat him with respect.

Although, he had been permitted to pursue his Ph. D degree by his family, yet he had to seek the recommendation of one of his teachers in M. A. for his acceptance by the university. It so happened that the IDIOT went to all the university Professors with his publications as his credentials for his acceptance as a research scholar but all of them cut a sorry figure saying that they had already registered six research scholars as per rules and also pointed out indirectly that the HOD had still a provision for one research scholar under him. The hero was neither the son of a publisher, nor of any Minister, nor was he a beautiful young girl whom the HOD could favour. As a result, he returned highly dejected. One day when he revealed his sorrows and tensions to one of his well-connected teachers in M. A., he doesn't know why he took pity on the idiocy of this IDIOT and promised to get the job done. Knowing well the truth of his high recommendation, family background, his hard work and intelligence, the HOD put him off three or four times and then he called him to his office once and tried to prevail upon him saying, "Of what use will the Ph. D be to you? Pity yourself. Take pity on your weak vision. You have to study a lot during research. You won't be able to endure this strain. You belong to a well-off family. Why should you need it? Run your cinema house leisurely. What is there in research work? Fulfill yourself in your writings. You are a born creative writer, why do you want to waste your capability in research work? Don't take ill whatever I have said to you, do reflect on it." Our hero kept listening to all this with his head hanging down. He felt as if somebody was throwing acid on him drop by drop and is not allowing him even to complain. He realized it many times because he had to listen to these dialogues from the mouth of the HOD. He felt utterly despondent. He felt that his dream of becoming a doctor shall never be fulfilled, he won't be able to honour his promise given to his "inspiration". He felt that there were everywhere social boundaries he won't ever be able to break. It was all beyond him why the whole society was hostile to him. The stupidest are allowed to move forward, the most stupid student is permitted to take up research, he alone is there who is humiliated everywhere because of his high-powered glasses in spite of his all hard work and intelligence. Why so? He was unable to understand the objection of the HOD to allow him to take up research. Friends, who will convince that IDIOT that he has nothing to give to the HOD whereas that serpentine-eyed beauty who is an obstacle in his way has the treasures to offer to the HOD and due to whom he is putting off the hero. Of course, if the HOD had been a gay with the hero's interest in it, he would not have been allowed to join research but also got the readymade thesis. Well, our hero remained adamant and that serpentine-eyed beauty allowed to work on a simple topic and in her joy of getting an IAS officer, didn't show any favour to the HOD. In his humiliation, the HOD signed the papers of the IDIOT but in order to teach him a lesson, he gave him a difficult and unfamiliar topic for research which a scholar of ordinary intelligence would have given up in a few months. But our hero was after all the IDIOT! He was overjoyed and devoted himself to the task. He did overcome the difficulties of the research work but his exploitation by the HOD was intolerable for him. He swallowed this bitter drought also because he was to realize his dream. He had learnt this truth that struggle alone is his mindset and the heroine his inspiration to face the struggle continuously.

In spite of all this, if the hero had any pain and yearning, it was that he had nobody to share his happiness. Whenever he was blessed with any success, his happiness changed into sadness thinking that she with whom he wants to share it and who would be extremely delighted to know this, is far away lost in her domestic life. He was doing all this for his 'inspiration', he was keeping his promise only. He had never enjoyed his happiness whole-heartedly, this yearning teased him all his life.

Every time, he shared it with his 'inspiration' and felt happy to see her happy. This was the only way with the IDIOT to celebrate his happiness. He was not sad that none remembered him but he was sad why the memory of some haunted him.

Sometimes he had a painful realization of his being lonely. Even then, he didn't think of making anyone his companion. If there was at all a talk of his marriage, he would put it off saying that he had yet to stand on his own feet. The hero didn't know how and why it went deep into his mind that the way the heroine loved him, what she is, there can be none like her nor anyone can love her. This fixation of the hero forbade all girls to stay away from him. If at all some came, the hero discarded her comparing her with the heroine. Secondly, it was the wish of that inferiority-ridden hero that someone should love him – even after being accepted by the heroine, he began to believe again that nobody can love him. So he didn't get closer to anybody. Thirdly, he wanted to escape the situation after being hurt by the heroine. His heightened emotionality wanted to save him from a fresh scar. He had bound himself to the commitment he had given to his 'inspiration'. That IDIOT couldn't understand that the girl has to be wooed, she herself never takes the initiative. One has to flatter her a little, what we call admiration in decent language, only then she lifts the wooer a bit. Otherwise the girls have become so advanced that they succeed in winning over the boys they like. They do this wisely for a happier future keeping in mind the fascination of the handsomeness and wealth of the boy. Our hero could never project himself properly inspite of his well-off family and his own brilliant capability. He could have done this all, or the story-teller could have projected this, but was unable to accept anybody with the adoration of his heroine. His heroine thus bound him tightly.

In those days, some friends of the hero who loved him and were annoyed with his self-centredness, silence, self-suppression and ignoring the girls, conspired to liberate him. They took him on a tour to Jaipur in a car. They wanted the hero to be somewhat normal. They took him to an old dirty house where old vulgar women chewing betel leaves and chattering indecently and nakedly, shocked and puzzled him. One of his friends paid five hundred rupees to a good-looking girl for his sexual enjoyment and pushed the hero with her into a room. He happened to find himself in a small room with a lighted bulb. There was a charpoy with a sheet spread over it in the centre. That beautiful-looking girl shut the door and caught him by the arm and seated him there. She took off her clothes gracefully one by one to excite the hero's passion. She was advancing to embrace him when he pushed her away and ran out of the room wiping the perspiration from his forehead.

I know that the readers would raise their eyebrows saying – "The anger of the Hindi story-teller marred by idealism." I heartily accept your charge but dear friends! Believe me I wanted it myself that the hero should enjoy all these pleasures there for which I had taken him there. We would have got the evidence of his sexual potency if he had done this all – and the Hindi story-teller would also have been saved from this allegation. But it so happened that the hero pushed me and ran out also first time like that girl. He himself is responsible for this foolish behaviour, not me at all. Had I got an opportunity, I wouldn't have left that girl without my roused passions satisfied with all the risk of being afflicted with syphillis later.

Now the question is why did the hero do all that? How can I answer this? he didn't seek my permission to do so. I'm giving here the opinion of some so-called mature readers, you may conclude yourself. At first, the hero was not mentally prepared for this enjoyment. Suddenly, he was pushed into that situation. Secondly the aesthetic sense of the hero was hurt who had been enjoying his childhood with the fairies, youth with the film heroines and then his life with his beautiful heroine with a melodious voice. Thirdly, he felt that with that act of passionate enjoyment, he would fall from the eyes of the heroine for ever. Then he won't be able to forgive himself. Fourthly, he is a boy from well-off family with noble values.

Whatever it might be, this incident might have raised the hero in your eyes, he has fallen forever in my eyes. Such IDIOTS are not welcome now as characters. Readers, the hero didn't do well by pushing his story-teller. Does anybody push away his elder, his father? The way he has hurt me, I must avenge myself on him. If he is a son born in this Kaliyuga, I too am a father from that age. Such a foolish dreamer must be punished for his action. I'm looking for an opportunity. I have got him pulled up and reproached by his friends. He was very unhappy at this and I have kept the thought of revenge in my unconscious to see what does the hero do next?

The story of his struggle is very long to earn his livelihood during the course of his Ph. D and afterwards. It may take countless pages if I narrate it here. His struggle was hard. Even after learning the harsher realities of the world and gaining wisdom, he didn't give up his basic nature. He neither knew anything about the art of cunning, sycophancy and bribery nor did he want to know. Above all, he was fully confident of his deep and vast studies, his basic thinking and abilities. In such a situation, struggle is natural because the people in power in this country think it better to appoint dullards as professors instead of finding brilliant youngmen for such positions so that the authority of these frogs in the well (Stagnant narrow-minded) may remain secure. He was sick of appearing for the interviews. He was asked to meet the President of the college. He took it as personal humiliation to talk and flatter a matric-failed ordinary shopkeeper selling mustard oil President of the college. He didn't go there to see him as such. He didn't contact even a couple of HODs annoyed by their nasty attitude. It astonished and shocked him to think why he was denied the job with his abilities and capabilities whereas the individuals with lower caliber were appointed. He never suffered a setback or cut a sorry figure in the interview. He was always successful from this angle – even then, he was considered inferior. Who could convince that IDIOT that his greatest fault was his honesty, intelligence and capability? This country doesn't need them in spite of their loud proclamations for such preferences day and night! This country has been run and is being run without the brilliant, honest, capable and hardworking. Interview is a mere formality and a mockery and I am expressing the deep anguish of that IDIOT with an example of this thorny reality. (Those who have passed through such disgusting realities must be well familiar to give more interesting examples.) A female candidate was asked in an interview, "What does *Khadi Boli*(spoken language of the rustics)?" that girl answered in her own grace and art, "The one which is spoken while standing!" the panel of the wise learned sages of the present times, pleased with the artful grace of that girl, selected her for the position of a professor. In such a situation, the IDIOT hero was unwanted. He was already tense in his empty life and this struggle further shattered him. Only a few friends of his were there to keep up his courage and spirits. He kept fighting for five years against this professional setup and also troubled by the taunts of the family. He thought of committing suicide. This time, the inspiration of his 'inspiration' couldn't calm him down. He would talk to his heroine in monologues only. There was none who could tell him not to feel broken even in this situation.

Since he had to see more of life's rut and rot, he succeeded in getting the petty job of a professor after fivers of hard struggle. He was happy and so were the members of his family. He missed only his mother who would have made a 1.25 rupee offering to the idols in the temple. Here there was missing his 'inspiration' who had motivated him to reach this position. The hero again endured the pain of his inability to reach them. He had submitted himself to the situation. His loneliness had become an essential part of his life from which separation was unimaginable. His struggle to establish his identity and gain respect in society had somewhat come to an end. His struggle to control and discipline the pack of monkeys in his classes still continued because of his weak vision. The hero had a continuous feeling that he was born to struggle only.

Immediately after getting a job, the hero decided to realize his long-woven dream. In fact, whenever he felt the need of some shelter during the hard struggle of his life, he read the long letter packed with emotions written to him by the heroine, embraced it and felt considerable relief. But now he had begun to realize that the heroine had forgotten him to lose herself in her domestic life. It pained him deeply to think that someone else had a right on the heroine's love. This thought irritated him, made him uneasy and restless, that his 'inspiration' was in someone else's arms. He is longing to share his sorrow and he imagined his heroine smiling, talking, laughing and loving her husband. The hero couldn't have any way out but torturing himself with such thoughts. He felt jealous of that unseen lover. This desire was on the verge of madness in him to remind his heroine of him that somebody is still alone and sad and has the same love for her even today and a prey to a queer wait for her and thus deeply tense. He happened to trap a publisher to fulfil his desire and gave him his poetry book for publication. The hero dedicated this book to his heroine.

The publication of his first book didn't delight the hero as much as the thought of finding the whereabouts of the heroine to send her his book. He had been yearning for long to write a letter to the heroine. He had written her a letter many times in his thoughts. With this strong desire to be fulfilled and full of enthusiasm and a beating heart, he reached the home of the heroine after a long time where he had gone once or twice when the heroine was there. The heroine's mother welcomed him in the living room and herself went to the kitchen to make tea for him. The loneliness of the drawing room was extremely painful for him. He had been yet experiencing the haunt of memories when his eyes fell on the smiling picture of the heroine and it shook him. He was badly shaken on seeing the heroine after a very long time, may be in the picture. He now realized his own poverty that he didn't have even a picture of the heroine. Another picture beside that of the heroine in the drawing room was an eye-sore to him and he didn't look at it again. How could he tolerate his rival? The stitched wounds of the hero began to crack one by one on seeing that smiling beautiful picture. The sharpness of the loneliness and tragedy of his life was piercing through and tearing at him. A deep sigh escaped the hero on seeing that picture. His heart cried at her smiling face. He felt like crying there and then. A thorny jungle cropped up in him that was piercing through his body. But his heroine was smiling. The hero repented at his coming to this home. The hero was feeling helpless and thoughtless at his overwhelming emotions. With his eyes fixed at that picture, he didn't know what to do.

Unaware of the hero's refreshed wounds, the heroine's mother kept pouring salt over his wounds with the pieces of happy information – she has visited home five times, she has beautiful children, her husband earns a lot etc. etc. the hero was listening and each information made his inner self cry. Even after taking tea there as a poison, he came out as if he had thrown away all his own. That IDIOT kept hurting himself with the arrows of questions at himself on the way. His condition was pitiable. The heroine didn't meet him even after her five visits and he wasted half of his life in wait for her. He had never thought that the heroine would forget him so easily and dash his penance to the ground like this. What did he expect from the heroine? Only this that the heroine should have enquired about his well-being and thrown away some pebble-like words as an aim, just to keep up his courage, in his worn-out *jholi*. This alone would have been enough for him. The heroine didn't do this even. His whole life is gone to pieces, the hero felt. He surrendered himself completely to keep his word and there is that heroine who didn't deem it proper to know his well-being. He is dead for the heroine. Does anybody die so easily in memories? There couldn't have been so hard a compulsion that she she didn't have even five minutes for him. The fact is that the priorities of the heroine have changed. The hero is no longer a part of her life, not even of her memories as she had got all that she desired. And he staked all his life in another illusion. How else to address him, if not an IDIOT?

The happiness and excitement of the publication of the book changed into deep sorrow. Mental tension overpowered him. He lost both his appetite and sleep. All night he moved about the room and smoked cigarettes. Even after sinking himself in drinking, he couldn't free himself from the question how the heroine could forget him. How did he lose the very basis of life? What should he do with his life? He was alive only on the hope that the heroine remembered him.; loved him still; she is not able to meet as she is far away, otherwise she too wants to meet him. He crossed all the hurdles of his life on the hope that his heroine is still there in his life. But she has thrown him out as a fly is thrown out of the milk. The smiling face of his heroine appeared before him and he wept at his own helplessness, inability and dejection.

Our IDIOT hero remained down with depression for many days. Tense and sorrow-stricken, he was making an unsuccessful attempt at forgetting everything by drinking in excess. The callous movement of life was of no good to him. He had been deprived of the very basis of his life. That emotion-packed letter of the heroine had become an agonising question-mark. His friends took him to the doctor. When he came a little out of depression, that IDIOT started thinking that he had done grave injustice to the heroine by believing all that the heroine's mother had told him. What does her mother know about the mind of the heroine? Who knows anything about someone's inner wounds? He also laughs all the time. Who knows about the lava bursting continuously in his bosom? What does the heroine suppress in her heart cannot be known from her smiling behaviour to cope with the worldly life. Nobody knows anything about her compulsion for not meeting the hero. May be she didn't come to meet him thinking that his happiness would be disturbed. He must send his book to the heroine. Even if she has forgotten him, he must tell her that she is still his anchor, his 'inspiration'. The heroine will surely respond in her own way. That will bring out the whole truth. He wrote a letter thrice only to be torn into pieces. At last, whatever he wrote as a short letter, is this –

"I'm sure that this letter of mine will not only shock you but also disturb you to think from where this dead person has risen from the world of oblivion. I would never have created an obstacle in your smoothly flowing life if I were not to send you my published book out of my only adamancy to keep my promise. If I had not done so, I would have either destroyed these compositions or they would have been eaten by termite.

"You may say that if I have been doing all this, you have nothing to do with it. After sending the book, what was the need of this letter? Both these points have a correctness of their own. I don't want to rely to the first in this letter. I am writing this letter in reply to the second.

"This book is dedicated to you. There were many lines written on you when I wrote the dedication but, with many considerations, I deleted all but one. Reason? The society has nothing to do with my personal life. However, I had a mind to express my gratitude to you, may not be in the book, I must do so individually. But shall I be able to say all I want to? I don't think so.

"I have lived my life quite wrongly. If there was any good or meaningful in this wrong and foolish life, it was your sense of belonging with me which I may not evaluate properly. Now when I see only sands to a distance in this scorching heat, only one feeling gives me relief that you recognized my mental abilities and encouraged me to refine it, inspired me which could not fructify into fulfillment because of the poisonous relations and tensions. Helplessness to live is left alone because everybody doesn't have the courage to die. I feel sad that I couldn't fulfill your hope. I beg to be excused for this that I could not express my gratitude to you as much as I should have.

"I shall be grateful if you give your opinion on the book. Do acknowledge its receipt if you couldn't do that. It will be a mental consolation that what was yours has reached you. It has been the only advantage of the book that I longed to write a letter to you that has been fulfilled.

"Pretend sometimes to remember this poor fellow – I have heard that the housewives are quite good at it.

"Best wishes to all in the family.

Should I expect a reply to this letter?"

This letter of the hero shows his deep sorrow, disappointment, anger and inspiration. Now he found it difficult to write something on the book. He remembered a number of Urdu couplets which were expressive of his mental condition. He liked very much an Urdu couplet of Zubair Rizvi which suggested many aspects of his situation-

"I have also looked for no companion after separation from you,
Look far into the crowd and see me alone."

But how could this IDIOT quote another's couplet when he quoted his own in his wooing. Then he wrote this couplet-

"Even now in darkness, it shows me the path,
What you talked is all a light!"

Thereafter started the wait for the heroine's reply. He would be extremely delighted to see in imagination the heroine holding his book, in boundless joy and then a layer of sorrow on her face. He was sure of the heroine's beautiful inspiring reply. He imagined that and felt happy to think of the words therein. Time rolled on and the hero's unease also increased. The postman was quite surprised to think why the hero so highly educated, intelligent and advancing in years was showing childish restlessness for a letter. Hero's restlessness began to change into sadness. Even his book seemed to be ill-omened to him. Will he lose this last hope also? How will he survive then? He would make himself tense with such reflections.

Naturally, the letter will take its own time. One day, he received it also. Now look at the condition of the hero. Reading his own name in the heroine's hand, he felt as if she had touched him lovingly after a long time. He opened that letter with a beating heart. He received the first hurt on opening the letter was that this letter was writtten in few lines as against his expectation for a long letter. He began to read it with a saddened heart:

"I don't know how to express in words my delight I have felt on receiving your book? My prayer to God is that you keep progressing like this by leaps and bounds day and night and keep remembering me as such.

"I have read some poems and hope to read soon all the poems in my friend's collection and try to understand the experiences of a friend who occupies some space even today in my heart.

"I have not written a letter to anyone for quite a long time – please excuse me.

"Take care of yourself.

Yours!"

This balanced letter of that true housewife which gave many hints dashed all hopes of that SUPREME IDIOT. It added to his tension. He felt broken-hearted. It seemed to him that his heroine had forgotten him. He read that letter a number of times. He tried to find something in those lines for himself but returned empty-handed. He wondered to think that she couldn't write even a line on hero's letter. Has he received the letter or it has been stolen? Has she really lost all interest in hero's book? Why did she pray to God for his progress and not gave him inspiration directly? The hero tried to read the meaning of his desire in every line of the letter and returned disappointed. It troubled him to think why the heroine knowing it well that she was the very basis of his life and each word of her was a drop of nectar, should be so indifferent? To be brief, there was only one line that was a straw for a drowning man, for the hero-"He still occupies a space in some corner of the heart." This also troubled him that "He still is there in some corner of the heart." It means that he was no more a part of her memories. The hero is a forgotten dream now. He was right that the heroine had forgotten him. As his this belief became stronger, it disheartened him. It seemed to him that the basis of his life is shaken. He staked all his life for the heroine – and this is the reward? He kept this letter with that letter of the heroine which still was his life-giving force and then dejected, broken, lifeless and tense he sat as if he had returned after losing a great battle. His dream had been shattered. Angry with himself in that broken condition, he tore into pieces some of his compositions. But now there was none whom he could send these torn pieces in an envelope to somebody and these adored the dustbin. That IDIOT should have been thankful that the heroine remembered him at least and didn't forget him like the rags thrown away. Even now, she addressed the hero as a friend and didn't treat him as a 'brother' as it is the custom after marriage. The heroine didn't show the conduct of those saintly women who forget not only the complexion but also the name of their lovers after enjoying the embraces of their husband. But that great IDIOT couldn't understand the restrained language of that faithful housewife and suffer a new wound on the ageing life.

This IDIOT again went into depression. This time, the depression continued for months and was painful. This time, there was nobody around him to comfort him like before and he had no logic. The pain of his life gone baseless began to pierce him. When he took courage this time to come out of this acute mental tension, his eyes opened into the continuous dreams of childhood and found himself not only all alone but also that the journey of life ahead was more scary. For the first time, he realized the warning of his friends that his weak vision would be more problematic in future. His brother and *bhabhi* won't stand by him all his life; they have their own interests and their own family. What would he do then? He should have some companion. He realized it for the first time that his ideal one-sided love was only a lie, madness and an illusion in which he has ruined the best part of his life. He realized that his love was one-sided – he was dead for the heroine since long. What is this love that one lives one's life yearning, longing and languishing every moment of life and the other unaware of this enjoys the passion of life in the lap and embraces of the husband or wife. The hero felt a strange dispassion for this one-sided love. It seemed to him that he was one of those unfortunate people with both the hands empty. He was dead to love; he endured this pain also by himself. For the time, broken by the heroine's letter, broken and defeated, this IDIOT was completely disheartened and despondent and surrendered himself to the pressure to go in for marriage.

Then started the search for a match for this middle-aged poet, IDIOT, stubborn, simple-minded Professor's marriage. This requirement was advertised, the friends were also requested. This experience was very bitter for the hero. I don't have the capability to acquaint the readers with every incident and here are some of the hero's experiences that would satisfies me and also satisfy the readers. It should be remembered in view of these instances that the hero being highly emotional, impractical, living his life in the ocean of beauty, howsoever in illusions he might have been, is the only lover who loves the heroine even after being hurt for the second time.

- He was shown a girl who looked like his mother in health and physique. Her face was wrinkled and her cheeks had shriveled flesh. Her complexion was a little dark. That girl said that marriage for her meant abandoning her parents. She demanded that the hero must learn how to drive a scooter. The hero was in shock for many days after seeing that horrible face.
- He was shown another girl whose cheeks were pressed as the mango after its seed had been taken out. And then her make-up on it gave her horrible appearance.
- He was shown a girl who was beautiful indeed but a friend told him that he needn't marry her as she is available just for a thousand rupees.

If the hero rejected such half a dozen girls, there were more than a dozen girls who rejected the hero for his high-numbered glasses. He couldn't see another fifteen girls because their parents had rejected him. The largest number was of such people who took the horoscope of the hero but didn't return. It astonished the hero that the combination of Rahu, Mars and Saturn in the first house of his horoscope alone had made him vulnerable. Why does an astrologer tell from his horoscope that he is extremely gentle, truthful, honest and sensitive; that he is not stupid, cunning, cheat, cruel and has no greed for dowry. Even when the marriages are solemnized after tallying the horoscopes, the wives are burnt, beaten by the mother-in-law and father-in-law, tortured by the husbands, sold, deserted, raped, used as a tool for the immorality of husbands, sold with the thistles of taunts if bear a female child. The hero not only laughed but also became angry at the orthodoxy of the people. But he could do nothing for the people fond of living like beasts.

The truth is that whereas all wanted him to be married because of his weak eye-sight and the same weak eye-sight was an obstacle in his marriage. Even his brother and his wife never wanted him to be married; so they used this reading and conclusion of pundits as a shield to ignore the issue of his marriage. Who can stop the horoscope reading from being wrong when there is no effort? He was asked to get a false horoscope but our idealistic IDIOT was not ready for this crookedness. My readers can question here that it is not possible that hero didn't receive any proposal for marriage. There must be at least two or three proposals, are all fathers foolish? Sometimes, the comments of the readers are more rational than that of critics, especially Hindi critics. Respecting this comment of the readers, the story-teller would like to mention only two such proposals here in brief. Once after seeing the hero secretly, a gentleman father happened to see the hero's father. The hero's father who was dependent and was at the mercy of his daughter-in-law after the death of his wife, had to dance to the tunes of the daughter-in-law. In view of this weakness, he also told the father of the girl that his son's weak vision is a curse for his marriage. The father of the girl felt disheartened and returned. The hero never knew about this episode. Had he known it, who knows how he would have taken it. In the second proposal, the father of the girl was happy and agreed and assured that his daughter would certainly like the hero but the hero should once appear before his stupid, obstinate and arrogant wife in ordinary glasses. This proposal angered our hero. He bluntly refused to do so. Who can think of the well-being of such an IDIOT, friends?

The hero was all by himself again with all his old problems and tensions. Whatever he had achieved in his life was on his own strength. He sought help from none. He was disappointed if at all he sought help from anybody. In spite of this, his own zeal and passion kept him alive. He was active in his daily life. He was discussed in the field of literature but not much as he has wished. He could not be considered the best even after treating respectfully the live woman for all women obviously are the different forms of the heroine. The reason is that he kept himself away from the politics of literature in his idiocy. He never either pampered any critic or befriended a litterateur thinking that he is associated with any literary institution and shall help him in winning an award. He never wrote himself the review of any of his books. Whoever wrote anything, he accepted it even if he was not satisfied. He never either pampered any go-between to participate in the poetic recitations or offered his compensation or a beautiful girl to the organizers or managers of such functions. He was deeply pained to observe that the litterateurs and poets showing its ugliness to society had relations with their fellows based on jealousy and malice. Self-idolizing litterateurs do not like to read, what to talk of appreciation, the better creation of any other poet or writer. They do not miss an opportunity and use mean and dirty politics to disgrace and degrade the creations of fellow writers. He was all the more astonished to learn that the poets were not only habitual of reciting the stolen couplets of one another, but there were some would take the compositions of anonymous poets on payment, recited them as their own to achieve the status of a renowned poet, and have also published their books. Even today when some poets go to participate in the poetic recitations, they carry with them their disciples or apprentices and themselves usurp the monetary gains or compensations of their participating disciples – obviously the *ghazals* of these disciples are also their own compositions. Our hero observed that literature is no longer a harsh penance, but only a business like other businesses, in which one can't prove one's superiority without humiliating others. In this field also, groups actively operate like those in the political parties. It is necessary to be associated here also with some or the other faction to rise. Our hero's passion was broken. If he had known that the neat and clean beautiful temple of literature is also ruled by the hypocritical *sadhus,* the temple would have seemed dirty and disgusting. As such, he had to endure loneliness even in this field. He began to sharply realize the absurdity of life while reaching this age. He felt the futility of life, not his own but of others too. The reality of life's uselessness troubled him intensely. Sometimes he felt like running away from this life. His loneliness had been rising. He loved intensely the heroine even now but was completely broken somewhere after that letter. He felt tired and shattered. A strange feeling of asceticism began to overpower him. He often murmured the couplet of Salman Sayyad-

"Long endless walk has badly tired the traveler,
How long still is the journey is not known."

This uncertainty would keep him uneasy and restless. He felt life had lost its elixir – if at all it was there, it had gone dry or squeezed. He was always obsessed with the question of meaning of living such a life at all. Why has he come to this world? If there is any omnipotent power in which he has lost his faith why it has sent him to live such a life hither. What is its purpose? This question what he had gained after whole life's struggle also haunted him like an envenomed dead arrow. A petty job and negligible respect! Is it all the achievement of the whole life? Can it be called achievement? Achievement is surely zero. Millions have come and gone from here. Where are their accomplishments? What is the value of an individual in this boundless ocean of people? How can the accomplishment of a few be regarded as the accomplishments of all? Of what use is this purposeless life then? What has been the value and meaning of the life-long strife of the hero in this endless world without any essence? Hero's life had been entangled badly now in the questions? He would wake up at night with a start. All his night was spent in restlessly moving in the bed or moving about the room. He felt his emotions turning stony – he is becoming a hard intellectual. In such a situation, he would read the only letter of the heroine. This letter alone was capable of telling him that he still was emotionally strong even now. It is only a layer of snow on the flowing stream that begins to melt with a little warmth and the same clear clean flow of emotions begins. That letter was always hero's love as it was the only memory of the heroine. But this sweetness of some moments lay heavy on the bitterness of the rest of the time from which he was unable to liberate himself.

He had learnt the truth that life essentially is dull and absurd. Whatever attraction seems to be there, it is because of the charming but illusory warmth of relations. Perhaps that is the reason that an ordinary person badly entangled in it rarely realizes this truth. Perhaps that is the reason that when the warmth of these relations begin to cool down when we reach our middle age, people begin to take interest in religious rites and ceremonies to escape this dullness and dryness. They also set out on forming new relations. He found that people travel from one illusion to another all their life so that they can escape the naked sight of the meaningless life. He also learnt that the incantation of the formless Supreme proves more lasting as it has no danger of its shattering. His pain was that he had neither any relation nor any formless Supreme to live with illusions. He was completely helpless to watch the real, dry, harsh and callous form of life all alone. A strange feeling of belonging had originated in him. He had no interest in anything. Even then, he lived his life with a sense of commitment as he had not been able to break himself away from his 'inspiration'. Even now, this 'inspiration' was like a drop of the nectar of life while he was walking bare-footed on the burning sands in the scorching heat of life.

He had still been passing through these agonizing experiences of life when one day, his father died of heart failure. He was that father who had never given him his lap, never held his finger to teach him walking, never taught him anything, who rather always scolded him, hated him and left him to suffer and endure economic strains though he himself was quite well-off, never comforted him in troubled times even by caring to know the cause of his troubles, that IDIOT felt deep sorrow on his death as if he was uprooted. His loneliness was never that pointed sharp. There were many to show their sympathy and comfort but there was none to truly and genuinely console him. He was trying to solace himself. The very feeling of the father being there was a genuine comfort. Now he had been left with only his 'inspiration' who had already given him somewhere a deep wound.

He had not yet come out of this tragic shock when he came to learn that his brother and his wife had got the signatures of the father before his death on plain papers which they converted into his father's will with the help of a lawyer. The entire moveable and immoveable property of the late father had been transferred to his elder brother and his two sons. He was drowned in deep sorrow. It added to the tension of the IDIOT to think how these people who recite incantations and prayers to God twice or thrice a day saying 'empty-handed we come and empty-handed we go' could cheat their beloved ones. He was more shrunk and confined to think how much falsehood, hatred and blunt selfishness are hidden in all tall claims of belonging. His friends and sisters advised him to seek legal redress against this injustice with the full assurance of their support to him but he was a known IDIOT and remained so. He refused to go by their advice. He was not ready to come down to the level of his brother. He was not prepared to stoop so low for the wealth that is left here only after we are gone. When his father had no thought or feeling for him, who else is left to do so? Moreover, what will he do with this property? After enduring utmost economic hardships in life, he had lost all interest in the value of material wealth as ordinary people have. His brother had given the proof of his large-heartedness by taking pity on him and allowing him to stay all his life in the parental home but it created more agony for him to think what was the need for his brother to do this mean act when he was the legal owner of all property. If it was all that important, why did he not kill him with slow poisoning in the food? This would have averted the danger of his being alive and filing a suit against him. Who will convince that dunce that we Indians delight more in seeing others dying by inches than in killing them. In case of humans, our belief lies in slow killing than in killing there and then.

He just opened his eyes to see that here wealth not only involves the nearest, the dearest and the closest in litigation but also it leads to murders. The courts are loaded with such cases. They are lavishly wasting money to get money like mad, taking loans and borrowing while they talk of the ideals of Lord Ram and love! The essential basis of life is not love but money. Perhaps that has made life so disgusting. Money alone builds and breaks relationships. People are so shallow that they can only talk of love but they don't know how to live with love.

The emptiness of his life increased a little more. His sadness and pain deepened. He could never be like the people around him lost in hatred, jealousy, falsehood and fraud. He found the college professors good at everything except studies. They shared delights in maliciously harming their colleagues with the art of sycophancy. Such delights astonished the IDIOT? He found this disgusting form of these malicious pleasures wide-spread. The sight of all this made him more tense. He could never tell lies and people were not ready to listen to truth. He painfully realized that he was a misfit in this world. Why is he not like all though he is like all. This question was his piercing pain. He consistently felt that he had no right to live in this world. He found himself a stranger among the people. The feeling of his being a misfit added to his pains. He shared his pain with his few friends. They were also helpless even if they wanted to help. All have to carry their own cross. None can share the burden. This is an endless border nobody can cross and no spiritual power can show any miracle. The sufferings of others can be understood to some extent beyond which everybody is all alone. Such reflections engaged the hero in his loneliness. It seemed to him that he was al alone like Robinson Crusoe on this island-like earth.

Once again he woke up with a start at night. He couldn't understand it for some time, and when he understood it, he became tense to the extent of tension. This was the first night of his life when he had a dream without the heroine. Even the imagination of a dream without the heroine was an ill-omen for him. It was beyond him to think what all this indicates. His 'inspiration' alone had survived him even after being shattered by his 'inspiration'. The thought of a dream without hi 'inspiration' troubled him again and again while moving about the room.

After this incident, the hero had the worst days of his life because all his efforts to focus on writing failed him. The papers scattered in his room were expressive of his disquiet and his shattered inner being. Life had become an unbearable burden for the hero. He took all his life as the punishment of Sisyphus. Like Sisyphus, he went on struggling to push the stone up the steep slope knowing it well that it would be unsuccessful and all futile. He was not destined to hear a word love the whole of his life, not to speak of fulfilled love. He was alive even with that insatiable thirst concealed in himself only because his 'inspiration' was in his dreams and also lived in his writings. That night a dream without her made him sleepless and gave him torture and restlessness that were difficult to endure this time. Then he came to learn suddenly the meaning of a dream without his 'inspiration'. What is the meaning of living if 'inspiration' vanishes? When he understood it, there was left only one choice for him – suicide! He fulfilled his long-standing wish. He liberated himself from all his tensions, sufferings and setbacks. Since he was under the influence of cinema since his childhood, he chose the mode of death like that of Guru Dutt. He kept drinking the whole night in his room. The hurt of the heroine's disappearance from his dreams was such he knew nothing about drinking in excess. His life had no basis without heroine. And he died. Next morning, his family members found empty bottles and a glass with his dead body. How does it matter if one man whose identity is like that of a drop in the ocean goes? And the show of the world went on. Some genuine tears were shed which might have the immediate value but has no lasting value. The news of his suicide was published only in those newspapers which had either some space left for this news by chance or those which considered it more important than the news of rape or murder. The hero was not a petty politician on whose death the newspaper would have used a page or the Doordarshan arranged a special program or made a TV serial. He was only a litterateur, that too of insignificant language. What more reward can be there for the life-long struggle and creativity of a litterateur than negligible informative news to be easily forgotten? That IDIOT had known his own mind of treatment meted out to the earlier litterateurs by the inhuman, unenlightened and callous society. So he left this world without being a trouble to it. A couplet was surely found on his table which is mentioned for the delight of the readers-

I'm pained that all dreams are shattered but,
I'm happy that all dreams were pleasant!

Friends dear, the hero could have still lived because dreams never go stale, hopes never die. Otherwise too, billions of people live without any purpose and drag themselves. The hero too could have done the same. But I didn't let it happen so. My hero had pushed me out in that brothel house, in return for that, I had thrown him into the valley of death by demolishing the wall of life and mentally stunning him. I settled my score with him. I don't think any story-teller has ever killed his character like this. Sometimes you have to amputate your limb, many times you have to kill yourself. You take it in the same perspective. In other words, dear friends, what is the need of such IDIOTS and such category of people?

Of what use are such people as are physically handicapped or challenged, gentle, truth-loving, transparent in their words and deeds, harmless to others, unromantic, not exploitative or cruel or criminals, and good at keeping their word, have the desire to live their life honestly and dream of becoming Lord Ram or Bhagat Singh? What purpose will such people serve in this world? Today we need mentally challenged, liars, fraudulent, violent, stupid, dishonest, cheats, inhuman people to run this society. I wish that, not only in life but in the whole literature also, there should be no such IDIOTS, sensitive and innocent characters. That is why I killed such a character and proved it as suicide in the same way as people prove murders as suicide in daily life. I hate such characters from the core of my heart as are left with a little emotionality and humanity. Therefore I am in search of such characters as represent this brutal inhuman society and are not IDIOTS like the hero. HERE ENDS THE TALE OF THE IDIOT!

❖❖❖

Pre-publication Review of
A Tale of an IDIOT and Other Stories

by

Dr. Shaleen Kumar Singh
Head, Department of English,
Swami Shukdevand College, Shahjahanpur

A Tale of an Idiot and Other Stories, translated by R.K. Bhushan Sabharwal is a charming collection of short stories of Dr. Rajinder Singh Toki, a prolific writer of Hindi with dozens of published books to his credit. The present book contains 11 short stories of diverse yet delightful themes. All the stories of the collection are short stories, but the last story is the longest in size. The author/translator has arranged the stories in ascending order (in size), but each story is amusing, exciting, and gripping. The reviewing of these stories is also no less interesting as it amuses the reader to enjoy the fantastic translation of the veteran writer Prof. Bhushan on the one hand and to touch and feel the pulse of another senior author Dr. Toki.

The stories of the collection are near perfect from the viewpoint of themes, narrative technique, characterization, dialogues and the message it leaves to the reader. The plus point of Dr. Toki is that he has been translated with remarkable gravity and attentiveness; otherwise, sometimes, the translation mars the beauty of the text. The vast erudition of Prof Bhushan and his excellent command over both languages could make this strenuous task possible. The wide range of knowledge that Prof Bhushan possesses adds to the charm and intrigue of the stories. He even expands the world of the stories of rural and urban India. Here, the translation assists the reader in understanding the development of Indian society's values and cultural standards over the previous century and raise awareness of social injustices and economic disparities. In today's worldwide culture, the younger generation may understand historical injustice and societal imbalance. Such knowledge may help to recognise and address similar situations in the future.

Furthermore, the translator had maintained the distinct story-telling approach of the story writer. The underlying topic of each narrative of the story is about the struggles and tribulations and the defiance and perseverance of a poor man or a badly off section of society in the face of different nations' entrenched stereotypical ideas. Some women's economic disadvantages may result in extra problems.

Thus, the translator attains success in his attempt to relay the author's message as he translates from the source language without diluting the flavour of text by remaining vigilant constantly. Few critics and scholars of literature hold that usually source text is deeply rooted in its language, politics and society that the translator needs a proper engagement with the process of translation. Finding an appropriate equivalence from the source language to the target language is always an uphill task. One can translate words or speech, but one cannot decrypt emotions or feelings.

Another challenge is how to respond to the inevitable challenges. For example: What will a translator do if he/she comes across the local proverbs, idioms, or cultural-specific vocabulary? Will he/she be able to find an exact word, proverb or idiom in the target language or will he/she simply NOT translate that particular word or phrase?

Here Prof Bhushan adopts the second alternative. He doesn't translate the words so that people may not be misguided by the equivalent. We may take the following lines of the first story:

"Shut the door at least, yaar!" Said his friend lying in the bed.

Our hero's heart was fulfilled. He smoked another puff and shut the door."

Here, the translator does not translate the word "yaar" as there is NO appropriate equivalent in Yaar, so he leaves it.

The stories collected in the volume capture various social flaws prevalent in Indian society. Dr. Toki has lambasted these shortcomings and put forth them with emotion and pathos. The book deserves to be read by both thinkers and fiction lovers as it attracts people of both categories. The short narrative structure and the tough-tackling of the issue remain the prime concern of these stories. One can, however, imagine the shaping of the form of creativity within the author and translator's mind. The narrative structure is so well-knit that None can easily find fault with translation or original. Both are inalienably connected as both present before us a new take on the already much-discussed topics. Here one can glance at the images of poverty, nostalgia, social consciousness, and teaching-life are captured vividly by the fiction writer.

The book's stories are not restricted to a particular theme, historical era, or gender. The exploitation of the helpless by the strong is a topic that spans time, culture, and gender. Still, the oppressed and weak are typically seen as more susceptible in these stories. The stories titled Our Heroic Idol, SHRAADDH, ROMANCING WITH THE SHADOWS OF THE PAST, THE IMAGE IDEAL, SHRIMAAN JI?!!!, DEAD TO ALL SHAME – THE SHAMELESS, AMANUSHI, THE DENIED, THE DEPRIVED ∧ THE DESTITUTE are exemplary instances of the stories that broaden the horizons of the reader and let him/her reflect the kaleidoscopic angles of creativity and thought.

Dr. Toki's short stories collection and the unique translation of Prof Bhushan is unquestionably a vital contribution to the fields of Indian Literature and Indian Literature in translation. The majority of the chosen tales in the book highlight the various social, political, moral, and ethical issues and wish for a far better society for future generations. More translations like this are expected from a well-accomplished writer and the translator (Prof Bhushan) as it will assist in bringing the ideas of Hindi authors into the contemporary world. With best wishes.

❖❖❖

A Tale of an IDIOT and Other Stories: A Preview

by

Dr. Vandita Dharni*

Prof. R.K. Bhushan Sabharwal is an eminent educationist who has taught English Language and Literature, Communication Skills, Executive Communication to the graduate and post-graduate classes of Humanities, Management and Engineering Courses in different colleges and Institutes and Universities for more than four decades. He has also been a Visiting Professor and a Resource Person and a Course Writer. Prof. Bhushan has created a unique space for himself in Indian English Writing and Culture as a creative writer, poet, critic, research scholar and a book reviewer with 12 published books and about 40 research articles in reputed international journals.. His latest book *'A Tale of an IDIOT and Other Stories'* is a translation of Dr. R.S. Toki's book of Hindi short stories, *'Shraadh and Other Stories'*.

Dr. Toki is an intellectual giant, a renowned scholar, a critic, a poet, a short story writer and a philosopher with almost forty six published books. Prof. Bhushan's translation is steeped in a tradition and encompasses a rich spectrum of emotions – nostalgia, remorse and anguish evoked, seeps through the readers' sensibilities. These stories are about characters and situations from ordinary day to day life that reflect upon profound themes. Moreover, these stories deal honestly and truthfully with the existential issues facing absurd situations. The characters move on the course of life with their own commitments upholding the values they cherish in society in general and the story-writer is satirical in gently exposing the working of the powers that operate even on the educational campuses. His stories transport us from rickshaws to trains and finally to the fire that purifies the soul and consigns each mortal human to his inevitable death. But the journey doesn't terminate here.

Prof. Bhushan's translation of these stories into English is remarkably truthful and reveals his complete understanding of the content, spirit and style of the original. While reading these translated stories, we don't have even a remote feeling of translation and they have a genuine flavour of the original. The emotions, moods and moments in usual and tense situations with the response and reaction have been captured with extreme sensitivity in a clear and subtle language. This is no hoax translation. Prof. Bhushan fully understands the art of accurate translation and uses accurate and exact word and idioms, spoken and literal, as demanded by the characters and situations.

In the first story, we delve through nuances of an 'idol or self-proclaimed hero' who grapples with an existential crisis. The protagonist internalises his conflict in search for his true identity. He is shrouded by a deafening silence and Sartre's sentences in of 'Being and Nothingness' begin to chokes him. He associates himself with:

> *'A hero of Albert Camus he had admired also because he didn't remember even the day his mother had died.'*

Another poignant portrayal is of the demystification of a rickshaw puller in 'Rickshaw-Walla'. The intoxication of a *Mushayara* drenches the poet, Mr. Mehta on his way to the railway station when the rain pierces through his soul. The frustration of the sluggish rickshaw ride is overcome by the poverty and hopelessness of the languishing rickshaw puller whose wound is skin deep. It does not deter him from seeking prospective passengers to earn his livelihood even at the perilous risk of his leg being amputated due to gangrene. His wound becomes a motivation and not a crutch.

'Mr. Mehta felt relaxed as the rickshaw moved and he began to caress his ego remembering the applause of last week's Mushayara. He was hearing the dull sound of the rainfall and he felt lost in himself. The rickshaw was moving unbearably slow and Mr. Mehta took it as a blessing of the rains. In this mood, he didn't care for the jerks created by the rickshaw-puller's forced paddling, crying and his hand repeatedly pressing his knee on one side.'

The next story, 'Shraadh' illustrates Raghu's voracious appetite for books and Literature. The propensity of the rigid Brahmins towards rituals and tradition cannot be denied in context to the cultural milieu in which the story thrives. Raghu's offering a book as *dakshin*a to his guru only endorses this ideology. His devotion seems more appetising to the palette than even the mouth watering *kheer* or the guru *dakshina,* the book itself.

Shades of light and darkness are interspersed in the narratives which echo the writer's sentiments. The paralytic invalid confined to bed in 'Romancing With Shadows of the Past' is haunted by bitter memories of the past that shroud him with the guilt of being a passive observer when his wife Sulekha is emotionally traumatized by his parents and subjected to a deliberate and agonizing death due to an insatiable greed for dowry. Shards of remorse and a second wife's delusions leave him perplexed, bedridden and grappling with answers to the forbidden truth:

'As a result, his life of haste and waste had come to a standstill. He was experiencing living pain. Rest for a few days is a different matter but the agony of this very condition in future was increasing. God be thanked that he had enough money and means that he could employ a whole-time servant to take his full care. He was paying for neglecting his health.

This added to his suffering when somebody came to inquire about his health saying with a deep sigh-"Who knows of which bad deeds you are bearing this punishment today! You are only sixty." He would say ditto to them but in his heart of hearts, he was aware of the sin he had committed in his youth.'

The ticketless traveller Sunderlal's escapades in 'The Image Ideal' remain unhindered, despite his wife's vehement promptings. And he continues to indulge in delusional, paradoxical pleasures of travelling without a ticket. He is even confronted with awkwardness when he encounters an old student, Mangatrai who is a ticket conductor on the same train but he manages to camouflage his deception.

The opium effect of the beautiful girl and her poetry captivates the next protagonist who is a poet, hopeless romantic and '*a languishing Devdas*' as the writer calls him in 'The Spell of Creation'. News of her marriage proposals make him criticise the very institution of marriage to her but all his attempts are futile. She is oblivious to his surreptitious motives, gets married and revisits him years later with her child much to his dismay.

Another story that intrigues me in its sardonic flavour is that of the assertive Head of the Department of a college in 'Shreeman Ji?!!!' whose seething demands stem from an inferiority complex. He is envious of his bright student whose article on Shreeman Ji impresses him so much that he offers him a job opportunity that is yet to be explored. The poor scholar is left juggling with the enigma and possibilities that beckon him.

Another interesting character in 'Dead to All Shame – the Shameless' is the tactful sycophant Shyamlal who has no qualms in seeking a job for his daughter grounded on deception.

> *'The job of his daughter depended completely on his boss and his boss had assured him of appointment on the condition that she must have some published work. This shook Shyamlal for once but his expertise in telling lies prompted Shyamlal to say that his daughter is brilliant by God's blessing and that she has written a book at this age which is being published and that is why he wants her to be in job that may brighten the life of this innocent girl.'*

The story-writer asserts that '*Indian religion is an antidote to sexism*' and mulls over the multiple facets of a woman. He is of the conviction that she is as much to be blamed as her polygamous counterpart. The hypocritical obsession with religion takes precedence over marriage while men are prone to having an 'Oedipus' complex or mother fixation. The phobias and insecurities of Nirmal's mother obsessed with only sons is no longer a singular problem but a household saga. Her resistance to allopathic medicines was because of her ignorance and superstition. The orthodox ritualistic customs of smearing ash and drinking water of sacred rivers find a place in the narrative. Nirmal's mother's inevitable death, the pangs of guilt and his wife's indifference are commensurate with the theme of insensitivity and loss echoed in his earlier stories. He writes:

> *'This is the situation only of women, is not true. Some men are also a prey to 'mother fixation'. They keep crying-mother, O mother! Our country is a museum of such ironies. I vent my anger somewhat in my class or share it with my friend Nirmal who is also a voracious reader like me. He has also discarded all orthodox rituals like me. He is an ardent atheist and argumentative like me. He is more fortunate than me only in one way – that he hasn't married. He is bitterly opposed to the institution of marriage. He is not prepared to restrict his freedom even a bit.'*

The last story, 'The Denied, the Deprived and the Destitute' highlights the estrangement of brothers due to the unequal distribution of parental legacy which conjures up emotions, leaving the readers to contemplate on the adage, *'Wealth has wings'* – the harsh reality of life that wealth and materialism is but a mirage.

> *'He couldn't understand for which fault of his he had been thrown out so humiliatingly. He had an equal share in that one-crore home, fifty-lakh shop and fifty-lakh factory. But his flexible temperament and his lack of supine had transferred the whole property in the name of his elder brother and his wife under their influence and he had been ordered to leave home. When he called his married sisters to protest against this injustice with him, those kaliyugi sisters thinking that this unmarried school master will not be able to perform all the ceremonies on behalf of the maternal family at the time of the marriage of their daughters and worried about the same, they also stood by the elder brother. So he was left in the lurch with all his ideals, principles, honesty and his orthodox view of the relationships. He had tasted the naked disgusting truth of life for the first time and when he left home with the boxes packed with his books, his father or his brother and his wife had not gifted him even a piece of torn and dirty cloth to clean them, what to talk of a broken old pot or utensil.'*

Even the last story, the lengthiest, the title story, A Tale of an IDIOT, is satirical and ironical. We are told about the IDIOT, born almost blind for no fault of his own, was neither welcomed nor treated in the family. He was ridiculed by everyone and everyone in the family discouraged him in whatever he tried to do for himself. However, the courage, firm determination, grit and resolution of the IDIOT triumphed in his challenges to the cruel destiny and befooled all with his accomplishments. The reader may also join the general laugh and ridicule of the IDIOT initially but the success and achievements of the IDIOT amaze the reader that human will and grit can overcome the mountainous difficulties to win glory. Prof. Bhushan has used his translation skills deftly in conveying the truth of the original.

In brief, it can be said that Prof. R. K. Bhushan has added a fresh dimension to his creativity in translating these Hindi stories and the reader will certainly enjoy and wonder at his subtle understanding of the characters and situations in their social, family, educational, psychological and even cultural contexts communicated with his linguistic skills.

Happy reading!

❖❖❖

* (Dr. Vandita Dharni is a published poet who resides in Chandigarh, India. She has earned many a distinction in the literary field and has raised the bar by topping the University of Allahabad at the post-graduate level in English. Thereafter, she earned a Ph.D. degree in American Literature. Her articles, poems and short stories have been published in journals such as Criterion, Ruminations, GNOSIS, Hell Bound Publishing House, Borderless journal, RIC journal and International e-zines like Immagine and Poessia, Synchronised Chaos, Guido Gozzano, Silver Birch Press, Raven Cage, SETU, Fasihi, TSL Roseate Sonnets Anthology and Inner Child Press, U.S.A. She has published four solo anthologies, Quintessential Outpourings, The Oyster of Love, Rippling Overtures and An Alchemy of Musings. Her latest contributions include the Roseate Sonnet Anthology and Breathe Poetry anthology. She has co-edited anthologies such as 'The Petals of Peace' and 'Ruddy Ravens, Cheshire Cats and Rusty Rats' and has been honoured with several awards.)

Appreciation

Translation allows literature to travel, which means that writers can speak across generations and cultures. Bhushan achieves a delicate balance between being true to the original work while also creating something new and unique that evokes the same thoughts and sentiments. *A Tale of an Idiot & Other Stories* strengthens and benefits Indian writing in English, as a translated work, introducing new vocabulary and concepts. It's all about capturing the spirit of the original Hindi stories without literally translating them. The interplay between time, sentiments, place, and people is explored compassionately and expertly in this collection.

– Dr. Neeru Tandan

❖❖❖

Dr. Raghukul Bhushan, on the face of it, has made the most use of his literary caliber and experience in translating each and every nuance of the stories so that these stories can catch the fancy of the readers. He has successfully only transferred the beauty and soul of the original stories by Dr. Toki, in his beautiful translation – transcreation. Setting, characters, exposition, Actions, climax, conflicts (external and internal), resolution – all find an outstanding articulation and manifestation in this translational work. As for his translational skills, his translation of the stories must be assessed as accurate, consistent, readable, and of course, intelligible and are sure to be popular among the sensible readers of literature. Let's walk in the shadow of different realities fetched through the translational excellence by Dr. Raghukul Bhushan.

– Dr. Bhaskaranand Jha Bhaskar